SAVING THE SINGLE DAD DOC

LOUISA HEATON

MILLS & BOON

First published in Great Britain 2018
by Mills & Boon, an imprint of HarperCollins*Publishers*
1 London Bridge Street, London, SE1 9GF

Large Print edition 2018

© 2018 Louisa Heaton

ISBN: 978-0-263-07318-8

MIX
Paper from
responsible sources
FSC™ C007454

This book is produced from independently certified FSC™ paper to ensure responsible forest management. For more information visit www.harpercollins.co.uk/green.

Printed and bound in Great Britain
by CPI Group (UK) Ltd, Croydon, CR0 4YY

This item
latest dat
period if

- **Phone**
- **Visit wv**

    Disc

013855080X

Louisa Heaton lives on Hayling Island, Hampshire, with her husband, four children and a small zoo. She has worked in various roles in the health industry—most recently four years as a Community First Responder, answering 999 calls. When not writing Louisa enjoys other creative pursuits, including reading, quilting and patchwork—usually instead of the things she *ought* to be doing!

To Nan and Grandad,
whom we lost within weeks of each other.

It was way too soon and no one was ready.

This is for you.

CHAPTER ONE

'SO…YOU'RE GOING after all, then?'

Dr Bethan Monroe didn't need to look at her grandmother to know she was disappointed. She'd heard it in her voice. But what was she to do?

'I have to, Nanna.'

'No, you don't. Not with him. Not with a *Brodie*.'

Bethan groaned out loud. It really was quite childish, this feud her nanna had against that family. Okay, maybe not the *whole* family, but most definitely against one of them in particular. Thankfully the one she was seeing today was *not* her nanna's arch-nemesis—rather, he was his grandson.

'I do!' She stepped over to the kitchen table, snatched up the not insignificant pile of final demands in her fist and waved them about. 'Be-

cause if I don't then you lose the house. We had
the phone cut off last week for a whole day!'

Her exasperation wore off instantly when she
noted the discomfort on her beloved grandmother's face.

She softened her tone. 'Grace is in school now.
I can work again and pay my way.'

She'd missed it. Incredibly so. Being a doctor
was her calling and, though she'd loved being a
stay-at-home mum whilst her daughter grew to
school age, she felt a real yearning to get back
into the consulting room. It had always been the
plan that she would take this break, but she'd not
known how difficult it would be alone.

'But surely there must be other posts you could
apply for? Somewhere further afield? In Glencoe
or Fort William?'

Perhaps there were. But they lived *here* now. In
Gilloch. And she didn't want to be that far away
from her loved ones. Not any more. Grace was
growing up fast, and she didn't want her nanna
to miss any of it. Commuting for hours each day
simply wasn't on her agenda.

Living in Cornwall had been wonderful, but

that was in the past now. She'd returned to her proper home three years after Ashley had died. Back to the place she had been born. And it felt right. Coming home.

'This job—right here in the village—it's a gift in itself! I'll be able to get home whenever I'm needed. Say, if there was an emergency.'

She couldn't help but feel guilty once again as she thought back to when Ashley had died. For weeks she'd sat by his bed—keeping him company, holding his hand, reading to him, never missing a minute—and then one day she'd been called into work. There'd been an emergency—a train derailment—and all hands had been needed on deck.

And Ashley had died alone. She'd received the call at work, from a neighbour who'd had a key and had promised to keep an eye out. She'd not been able to get home quickly enough. Had got caught in endless traffic jams, delayed by lights and drivers who hadn't seemed to know which pedal the accelerator was.

She'd just wanted to get back to Grace. Pick her up from the childminder and hold her close against her heart before making that final walk into their bedroom, where Ashley had lain. She'd vowed never to be that far away ever again.

'It'll be okay, Nanna.'

Mhairi sank shakily into a seat by the table, adjusting the woven scarf at her neck. 'You have more faith than I. What that Angus Brodie put me through...'

'I know.'

'He ruined my life. I don't want to see another Brodie man ruin yours.'

'I might not even get the job.'

But she hoped she would. 'Brodie man' or not. They *needed* this! She'd only been back a few months and their financial situation was getting more dire. They couldn't live off Ashley's life insurance for ever.

This was about a job. Employment. That was all. It was a business transaction—not an affair of the heart. It wasn't going to be anything like what had happened between her nanna and Angus Brodie. Those had been different times back then. It was the past. And Bethan didn't feel she was ready for another relationship yet. She was over the raw pain of Ashley's death, yes, and she worried something rotten about raising Grace without a father figure around, but did that mean her heart was on the open market?

No. Not yet.

She kissed her nanna's soft, downy cheek and sat beside her at the kitchen table, one eye on the clock. 'We'll be okay.'

Nanna covered Bethan's hand with her own, more gnarly, liver-spotted one. 'I'm just so used to having you here now. I worry he'll hurt you, like Angus did me. But I'm just being a worry-wart, that's all.'

'It's in the past. Where it should belong. Let's look positively to the future. I'm a strong woman. I can handle myself and any Brodie male who even *tries* to cause me trouble.'

'Even handsome ones? That grandson of his... I've seen him about. I've seen how the young women of this village look at him. Like they could eat him alive!' Nanna smiled with reluctance.

'Even the good-looking ones.' She held her nanna's hand and squeezed it reassuringly.

Her grandmother smiled. 'I suppose I can't persuade you to become a sheep farmer instead?'

Bethan pretended to consider it. 'I'm not sure I'm an open-air kind of girl. Besides, wouldn't that be a waste of all my education?'

Nanna mock-doffed her cap. 'I don't know where you get it from. Your father loved to fish before he became a stablehand, and your mother enjoyed to sew…'

Bethan nodded. 'I *do* enjoy suturing.'

'Och, it's not the same and you know it!'

She got up from the table again and took the red bills from where Bethan had left them and went to switch on the kettle. She let out a heavy sigh, as if resigning herself to the fact that she was going to lose this battle of wills today.

'Okay…let's take a look at you.'

Bethan stood up, straightening her navy trouser suit and making sure her cream blouse was crease-free. 'Will I do?'

'He'd be a dunderheid to turn you down, lass.'

'Good.' She checked her watch. 'I'll be late. Will you be all right?'

''Course I will. I've looked after myself for

nearly twenty years—I think I can probably man-
age the next hour or so. Besides, I've had a few
orders come in for the shop, so I need to get those
bagged up.'

'Okay. Well…wish me luck?'

'Good luck, lassie.'

Bethan gave her a quick hug and one last look
that she hoped conveyed that everything would
be all right, and then she picked up her briefcase
and headed out of the door.

Nanna wasn't the only one who was doubtful
about expecting a Brodie to take her on. She'd
probably been the most surprised when a letter
had arrived, inviting her for an interview with
a Dr Cameron Brodie. But the past was the past
and she herself had no argument with the Brodies. Clearly Dr Cameron Brodie didn't have a
grudge either, or she wouldn't have been invited
for the interview.

Nanna's part-time job—dying her own rare
wool skeins to sell in an online shop—barely covered the bills, and in the last three months sales
hadn't been good. They'd struggled—and struggled hard. But now, with Grace having started

school full-time, Bethan had become free to get herself a proper job again.

She'd really missed work. She'd come home to start their lives afresh, and nothing could beat being a mother, but her whole heart had always wanted to care for others. There was something about being a GP that spoke to her. The way you could build a relationship with patients over years, so they wouldn't be strangers. It was a privilege to be a friend as well as a doctor, and although sometimes that was a difficult line to walk she did it anyway.

Helping people—healing them, curing them of their ailments—was a magical thing and something that she treasured. But the most she'd done over the last few years with Grace had been to patch scuffed knees, wipe snotty noses and nurse Grace through a particularly scratchy episode of chicken pox. The closest she'd got to medication was calamine lotion.

And what she'd been through prior to that, with Ashley, that had been... *Well, I don't regret a day of that.*

But he'd not been a patient, nor a friend. He'd

been her husband. Grace's father. Their relationship had been all-consuming in that last year, and she'd been bereft when he'd died. Quite unable to believe that she would still be able to get up and carry on each day without him.

But I did. For Grace.

She'd made the decision to move away from Cornwall three years afterwards, and coming back to Gilloch—to Nanna—had seemed the right thing. Mhairi was alone, too. She knew what the pain of losing a husband—and, sadly, a child—felt like. They were comrades in grief to start with.

But that was the past and now the future beckoned—and with it a fresh sense of purpose for Bethan. She felt it in her bones. This job—this interview—was the way forward for all of them.

As she strode through the streets of Gilloch, her head high and the strong breeze blowing her hair from her shoulders, she remembered Ashley's last words—*'You'll go on without me and you'll be absolutely fine.'*

She'd doubted it back then. That she would get through life without him. But time, as they said, was a great healer, and now she often found herself yearning for that kind of closeness again.

But she was absolutely sure—no matter how good-looking Dr Cameron Brodie was—that she would keep her work relationships on a different level from her personal ones.

Dr Cameron Brodie swallowed the tablets with a glass of water and hoped that his headache would pass. He'd woken with it pounding away in his skull and it had been a real struggle to open his eyes to the bright light of the early morning, to get up and get dressed to face the day. If it hadn't been for Rosie then he would no doubt have pulled the quilt over his head and gone back to sleep.

But it wasn't just Rosie. He had someone to interview today. Someone he hoped would take his place permanently at the Gilloch surgery. Not that she would realise that at first. He'd advertised it as a year's post. Twelve months—start to finish. But he knew that before those twelve months were up the people he left behind would have to rearrange their aspirations.

He had a ticking time bomb in his head. An inoperable glioma. And Dr Bethan Monroe had been the only applicant for the post. *Beggars can't be choosers.* Wasn't that what they said?

He made it to the surgery and opened up, having driven there wearing the strongest pair of sunglasses he owned. Sometimes in the early mornings the sunlight in Scotland could be so bright, so fierce, it would make your eyes water. The sun so low in the sky, its light reflecting off the wet road, was almost blinding.

The headache would ease soon. He knew that. The tablets his consultant had prescribed were excellent at doing their job.

And they allowed him to do his.

For a little while longer anyway.

He hoped that this Bethan character was a strong applicant. Her CV was impressive.

By all accounts in her last post she had started up a support group for people with anxiety and panic attacks. Somewhere for them to get together and share stories and ideas in the hope that they could learn that they were not alone in the fight. She had also put together a volunteer 'buddy system', for older people who were lonely to be paired up with a younger person who could be a friend and check in on them whenever it was needed.

Her references were glowing. Her previous colleagues and partners all sang her praises and had been sad to see her go. For 'personal reasons', whatever that meant.

He checked the time. If she was as punctual as she said she was in her CV, no doubt she would be arriving in the next ten minutes.

There was a small mirror above the sink in his room, and he quickly checked his reflection to make sure that he didn't look too rough— that there was some colour in his normally pale cheeks. That was the problem with being a red-head—he had such pale skin that when he was actually sick he looked deathly.

He rubbed his jawline, ruffling the short red bristles, and figured he'd have to do. There were some dark shadows beneath his eyes, but there was nothing he could do about those.

Cameron sat down in his chair and his gaze fell upon the one small picture of his daughter Rosie which he allowed on his desk. In it she sat on a beach, with the sun setting behind her and her long red hair over one shoulder as she smiled at him behind the camera. She'd put a flower behind her ear and begged him to take a picture.

She'd looked so much like her mother at that moment he'd almost been unable to do so. For a moment it had been as if Holly was looking back at him, smiling. She had simply taken his breath away that day. He had almost put the camera down.

'Daddy! Take my picture!'

He was doing this for *her*. It was all for Rosie now. They didn't have long left together and he wanted whatever time they had to be spent together, having fun and making memories, so that she remembered him long after he was gone. His voice, his laughter, how much he'd loved her, how much he'd wanted to spend time with her. He wanted her to know that she had been cherished and adored.

So it didn't matter if this Dr Bethan Monroe was a three-headed monster from Mars—he needed someone to take his place at the surgery and *soon*. If she was qualified, and didn't have a death sentence of her own, then she was going to be perfect for the job.

His phone buzzed. Janet from Reception. 'Aye?'

'Dr Bethan Monroe is here to see you.' Janet had put on her 'customer service' voice. It always made him smile when he heard it, because she somehow lost most of her Scottish brogue and sounded more English than anything.

'Thank you. Could you send her through?'

'Certainly, Doctor.'

He sucked in a breath and closed his eyes. Everything seemed so much easier when he took a moment to do that. Took a moment to meditate. To calm the body. Concentrate on his breathing.

Perhaps I ought to take up yoga? he thought with amusement.

There was a slight tap at the door.

He opened his eyes and stood up. 'Come in!'

Janet came in first, smiling, her bonny cheeks rosy-red. 'Dr Bethan Monroe for you. Can I get you both a pot of tea? Or coffee?'

He lifted his hand to demur, but then he caught

sight of the tall, willowy woman who had walked into his room behind his receptionist, her long, chocolatey locks of wavy hair flowing either side of her beautiful face, and he found himself unable to speak any words.

She was beautiful. Elegant. Elfin bone structure.

For a moment she looked startled, then she gathered her composure after seeing his no doubt deathly pale face and walked towards him and held out her hand. 'Very pleased to meet you.'

Now, she *did* have an English accent. A real one.

He suddenly became aware of his throat. His tongue. Had the temperature of the room increased? He felt hot, his mouth dry, but so he didn't give Janet too much fodder for the village grapevine he managed to force a smile himself and shake her hand. 'Hello, there.'

'Did you want tea, Doctors?' Janet persisted, looking from one to the other with wry amusement.

He hadn't wanted any before, but with his mouth this dry it might be a good idea. 'Er… aye…thank you, that would be great.'

Bethan Monroe nodded agreement. 'Thank you.'

'I'll be back in a moment, then.' And Janet hurried from the room, closing the door behind her.

He couldn't get over Bethan's eyes. As chocolate-brown as her hair, if not more so. She also had beautiful, creamy skin, with a hint of the English rose on her cheekbones and a wide, full-lipped mouth. She looked nothing like her grandmother, whom he knew well—even though she'd refused to be his patient for years and saw Dr McKellen instead, over in the next village.

You couldn't help but see the same faces out and about in Gilloch, and her grandmother, Mhairi, was well-known to him because of the upset between her and his grandfather years back, that probably no one except them ever talked about any more. He often saw her. She took long walks down to the wool mill, or along the front of the bay to sit outside the coffee shop, wrapped up in swathes of knitted garments and watching the fishermen come in with their catch.

'I'm Cameron. Very pleased to meet you.'

'Bethan. Likewise.'

'Please take a seat.'

She was long-limbed but graceful as she sank

into the seat opposite and laid her briefcase neatly against her chair. 'Thank you.'

'You found us all right?'

Clearly, or she wouldn't be here, idiot!

'I did. It's not far from my nanna's house. Well, *my* house, too, now, I guess.'

'You've been back in the area for a short while?'

'A few months, yes. I moved here from Cornwall.'

He nodded. Good. That was all good.

You're staring.

Cameron cleared his throat and stared down at her paperwork. The *only* application on his desk.

'So, we're here to discuss the vacancy of general practitioner here in Gilloch.'

He needed time to think. Time to reorganise his thoughts. He picked up her CV and read it through as if it were the first time.

'You're looking for a full-time post?'

'Yes.'

'And you've spent the last few years as a full-time mother? That's correct?'

'Yes.'

'You're aware that this post is very demand-

ing? Long hours—frequently past school pick-up
time—sometimes evening work, call-outs, home
visits, that kind of thing?'

Are you trying to scare her away?

She seemed to bristle slightly. Had he implied
that she wouldn't be able to cope because she had
a child? He hadn't meant to.

'What I mean is, it'll be an abrupt change from
what you're used to.'

'I don't think so at all. Being a mother is about
having demands made on you all the time—all
day long and sometimes through the night. There
are no days off. You can't go sick or take a holiday. You're always on call.' She smiled.

He nodded, seemingly unable to tear his gaze
away from her. There was something so vibrant
about her. So intriguing.

'You're absolutely right. I have a child myself.
Same age as...' he quickly scanned her personal
statement again '... Grace, is it?'

Bethan smiled. 'Yes. She's just started at Gilloch Infants' School.'

'So has Rosie. My daughter.'

She looked surprised. 'Which teacher does she have?'

'Mrs Carlisle.'

'Oh! They're in the same class, then.'

'I'm sure they'll become good friends.'

She smiled at him—a beautiful smile. 'Let's hope so.'

He considered her, enjoying her optimistic outlook. It had been a long time since he'd felt optimistic about anything, and it was just fascinating to see someone who shone so brightly with it. Surely there had to be shadows somewhere?

'It says here that you left your last post for personal reasons?'

'That's right.'

'Not because of the job itself?'

'No. I loved working as a GP, but my husband got sick and needed someone to look after him.'

'Oh. I'm very sorry to hear that. I hope he's better now?'

She looked down at the ground for a brief moment, her smile faltering, before she met his gaze again. 'He died. Of pancreatic cancer.'

He was shocked. And a little embarrassed at having pushed her to explain. 'I'm very sorry.'

'You weren't to know.'

'I lost my wife when Rosie was born. It's difficult being a single parent, isn't it?'

'I'm sorry, too. It can be, if you're truly on your own. That's why it's good to have family around.'

'Is that why you moved to Gilloch?'

'Yes, I was born here. Lived here in Gilloch until about the age of three or four, when my parents moved to Cornwall. My father was looking for better job prospects—my mother for better weather!'

She laughed at the personal memory and he loved the way her eyes lit up as she spoke of her parents.

'It was in Cornwall that I met my husband. He was a doctor, too. When he died I felt incredibly alone. My parents were gone by then, and I just felt a yearning to be with family. It's important, that connection. More than any other. We'd always kept in touch with my grandmother, speaking online and on the phone, and I wanted Grace to know her properly instead of just being a voice…an image. So I decided to move back here so we could look after each other.'

'Mhairi?'

She nodded.

Cameron put down her paperwork. 'Tell me what you think you can bring to this post.'

But at that moment there was another knock on the door and Janet was there, carefully balancing a tray with cups, saucers, a teapot and a small plate of biscuits.

'Thank you, Janet.' He dismissed her and waited for her to leave the room before turning his attention back to Bethan.

'I'm punctual, committed, hard-working. I'm good with patients and I know how to build a rapport with them. I believe myself to be very efficient, and I have a good talent for hearing what people *aren't* saying.'

Is that right?

'What would you say are your weaknesses?'

She shifted in her seat. 'I get attached. I care too much, too quickly, and don't always control my emotions.'

He frowned. That was a red flag. He didn't

need anyone getting attached to *him*! Even if it was just as a friend or a trusted colleague. He didn't need anyone to be hurt by his passing. It was going to be bad enough for Rosie. He needed strong people around to be there for her, not crying a river for their own pain.

'How do you mean?'

'It's the human element. I find it hard to create a professional distance sometimes. Especially with people that I feel I know well. I care for them. Feel for them. When they're hurting, so am I.'

She leaned forward, planted her elbows on his desk.

'What I mean is, if I've been looking after someone and then I have to deliver a shocking diagnosis that's going to affect their lives then I'm going to feel that pain with them. It will make me cry. Not whilst I'm *with* them,' she clarified. 'I'm not that unprofessional. But sometimes it can get a little bit too much.'

She looked at him with concern, as if she were worried she'd said too much.

'Actually, I'm not sure if that *is* a weakness.' She smiled. 'I think it just makes me human, and I think people *like* having doctors who aren't made of steel.'

She jutted out her chin, but didn't meet his gaze.

He suspected she thought she'd blown it.

She hadn't. Not at all. But she didn't know she was the only applicant, and she didn't know just how much he needed her. He *had* to employ her. No matter what. His time was running out. He would just keep his distance. As much as he could.

'I need someone who can take over my role completely. I'm leaving the practice for a year's sabbatical, to spend time with my wee girl, but obviously there will be a short transition period during which I will sit in with the new doctor and observe until they feel able to fly solo. How would you feel about that? Me looking over your shoulder?'

She nodded, smiling. 'That sounds fine.' Then she frowned. 'You're leaving? Completely?'

Cameron smiled. 'Completely. For a year,' he lied.

'Oh.'

Was she using that special skill of hers right now? Trying to work out what it was that he *wasn't* saying? Perhaps she was. He watched her observing him, looking for clues, trying to work out why a fully trained doctor would just leave like this, but he knew she wouldn't find the answer.

There were no outward signs of his death sentence. Just paleness and bags under his eyes, which lots of people had, and a slowly fading headache that she couldn't see. No one else knew either. Except family. He'd *had* to tell them. But everyone else just thought he'd been sick for a while and was now over it.

Cameron leaned forward and poured them both a cup of tea, standing up to pass her a cup and saucer.

'Thank you.'

'This practice has always worked well. There's a good team here. How would you make sure you'd fit in?'

She sipped from the teacup. 'I'm a local girl who's come home. I'm sure there will be lots of questions, which I'll do my best to answer honestly. You can't be a GP without having good people skills.'

He smiled. *Good.* 'Do you have any questions you'd like to ask me?'

Surely there had to be. All good interviewees were taught to ask something at this stage. To sound interested in the post, if nothing else.

Bethan stirred her drink and he noticed what fine hands she had. Lithe fingers, short nails with clear polish. He was struck by a sense of admiration for this woman. Her husband had died and she was a widow. A single parent like himself.

'There is one.'

'Aye?' He sipped his own tea, wincing at the heat of it upon his tongue.

'I'd like to know if I'd have full autonomy from day one? I know you'd be observing, but how long would you observe me for?'

He smiled. He *liked* this woman. She had spirit. And enthusiasm. And that mattered to him most of all. He was going to be leaving his patients in the care of someone else. Patients he had looked after for a good few years. He needed to know they were in good hands. She seemed a

steady, comforting individual. Someone who—
if he hadn't had this death sentence hanging over
him—he could imagine becoming great friends
with.

And for that reason he'd have to keep her at
arm's length whilst they worked together. Keep
everything brief and to the point.

'You'll have autonomy. And I'd like to observe
for two weeks.'

We won't get close.

'Two weeks...'

'Two weeks of me sitting in the corner and saying nothing. Unless you need me to, of course.'

She nodded. Smiled. 'That's okay by me.'

'Good.'

He decided to shock her. See how she dealt
with surprises.

'When would you like to start?'

She stood outside in the bright morning sun, a
little stunned.

I got the job!

Her first job application after a long break away!
Dr Brodie had seemed a very likeable man.

Handsome, tall, broad-shouldered... A typical Scot, if there was one, with that beautiful head of red hair. And his eyes... Such a piercing blue against those dark shadows that lurked beneath them.

Clearly he had not been sleeping well recently. Or he was worried about something. Was it his decision to take a year off? Was he concerned about leaving his patients with someone he didn't know? Perhaps there was something else. Something she didn't know yet.

It's none of my business.

What *was* her business, though, was the fact that she could start her new job next Monday! Cameron had said that Mondays were appointment days at the surgery. Tuesdays were for home visits, Wednesday was procedure day, when they'd perform small surgeries such as skin tag removal, wound care, that sort of thing, and Thursdays were for more appointments, as were Fridays.

Weekends and evenings were usually spent on call, but they shared the on-call with the practice over in the next village, so that they did actually get some time off on alternate weekends, and he'd said they didn't often get lots of call-outs.

Gilloch was a small coastal village in the Highlands. She could smell the brine in the air from wherever she stood. No more than a thousand people lived here and they were of sturdy stock. And now *she* would be their doctor.

Smiling, she set off back to her nanna's, to tell her the good news. She had no doubt at all that her grandmother would be suspicious about Cameron Brodie's motives, but Bethan was determined not to be!

I'm going to make this work. I'm going to make Cameron Brodie see that I am a brilliant doctor and that I will be able to care for all his patients as if he were still doing it himself! If not better!

She needed this. *Wanted* this.

And now it was in her grasp.

Life was changing now that she was back.

Just as she'd hoped it would.

CHAPTER TWO

'YOU'VE GOT YOUR phone in case I need you?'

'Yes, Nanna.'

'Your purse?'

'Of course.'

'You'll call me if anything goes wrong?'

Bethan laughed at her nanna's fussing. 'Why would anything go wrong?'

Nanna fiddled with the pendant at her neck. 'I don't know. I just have a bad feeling about this.'

Bethan held out her arms and scooped her grandmother into a hug. She needed one. She'd been nervous these last few days as her starting day had got closer. And Nanna was still utterly convinced it was all a great big trick to humiliate her further.

'It'll be okay. Dr Brodie is a very nice man.'

'Impossible! Brodie men are the *worst*.'

'Not this one. He's different.'

Nanna pulled back to look at her. 'You believe that?'

She smiled. 'I do. What happened between you and old Angus Brodie is ancient news.'

'Maybe to *you*.'

Bethan picked up her briefcase. 'You're all right getting Grace to school?'

Nanna smiled. 'Of course.'

'And picking her up at three?'

'Aye. I've a few orders to dye up today, but I'll remember. I'm not senile, you know.'

'I've told the school you'll be picking her up from now on.'

Nanna leaned against the kitchen sink. 'You're stalling.'

'I'm nervous.'

'You'll be absolutely fine. You're a wonderful doctor, lassie. The people here in Gilloch are lucky to have you.' She reached into her pocket and pulled out a small box tied with ribbon. 'I want you to have this.'

'What is it?'

'They were your mother's.'

Bethan opened the lid of the box and found inside a small pair of diamond earrings, sitting on a bed of red velvet. 'They're beautiful!'

'Your father gave them to your mother after she had you. I should have given them to you long ago, after you had Grace, but they're yours now.'

Bethan was touched. Such a wonderful gesture! She put them in and went to look in the mirror. Perfect.

'Thank you, Nanna.'

Mhairi smiled. 'Now, you go and show that Brodie boy who's boss!'

Bethan felt a little odd, knowing that she was in *his* seat and he was in a smaller chair right next to her as he showed her the ins and outs of the computer system.

She'd not said much to her nanna over the weekend, but Dr Brodie had been in her thoughts more than she'd let on.

Nanna was right. He *was* a handsome man, and when she'd first walked into that interview room she'd almost stalled, her mouth drying upon her first sight of him—this tall Scottish hunk, unfolding his long, rangy figure from behind the desk and stretching out a hand for her to shake. She'd felt sure he would notice the tremble that had begun in her body in response to him.

And now he kept reaching across the desk to point things out on the computer and he smelt *so* good! It had been a long time since she had felt aware of another man, and having one who smelt so great sitting right beside her was throwing her concentration slightly. Irritating her as she tried to fight it.

'So, if you want to print off some information about a condition, click on this box here, next to the diagnosis, and it links to a medical database. You see?'

He brought up an information sheet on scoliosis as an example.

She snapped back into professional mode. 'Perfect. And if I want to look up information on medication…?'

'Well, we have books, but if you click on that question mark next to the prescription box you can usually find what you need regarding the pharmacology.'

'That's wonderful. Thank you. It's pretty similar to the last system I used.'

'Any telephone calls with patients, any advice or queries, you mark them down in the patient notes—no matter how trivial. See the notepad icon? It all has to be logged. I find that helps with any possible discrepancies down the line, if they query anything.'

'Well, I hope there won't be any discrepancies. Not from me.'

'Excellent. Well, I think you're ready! Feel like meeting your first patient?'

She turned to look into his face, at those warm crystal-blue eyes of his that twinkled in his pale face, and felt a rush of heat hit her in the solar plexus.

Oh, boy, I'm in trouble!

'I am.'

'Well, just push that button there to call her in. Her name will come up on the screen in the waiting room.'

Bethan smiled, nervousness suddenly flooding her system. She adjusted her chair and let out a breath. Then pushed the button.

* * *

Mrs Percy was a sweet old lady who used a walker that she'd jazzed up with some fake flowers and pretty ribbons. She shuffled her way into the room and sat down with a satisfied sigh and a smile as she took in the two doctors facing her.

'Two for the price of one, eh? Lucky me.'

Bethan smiled. She liked her already. 'What can I do for you, Mrs Percy?'

She'd already checked her screen and observed that apart from some arthritis in her hips and knees, Mrs Percy didn't have much wrong with her. Blood pressure had been good on her last check and her cholesterol levels were low.

'I want to do the Edinburgh Half-Marathon,' she said, giving one firm nod as she delivered her surprising statement.

'You do?' Nothing could have surprised Bethan more. She'd maybe expected *My knees are giving me some gip* or *I'm not sleeping well at night.* Anything but what she'd actually said.

'Aye, I do. And they tell you, don't they—on the television and whatnot—that if you're about to embark on a new training regime or exercise you should consult your doctor? So that's why I'm here. Thought you'd better check me out so I don't drop dead halfway around.'

Cameron laughed beside her. 'Mrs Percy is our resident adrenaline junkie.'

Mrs Percy winked at him. 'Well, adrenaline keeps you going, doesn't it? I've seen those medical shows on TV, when someone's about to cork it and they give them a shot of adrenaline. *Brenda*, I tell myself, *you need some of that every day.*'

Bethan nodded. Fair enough! 'Okay…well, I guess we need to check you over, then. We'll need to take your blood pressure, listen to your heart, take your pulse. All right?'

'Aye, dear. You go for it.' Mrs Percy rolled up the sleeve of her vast knitted cardigan to reveal a scrawny arm. 'But I want a good answer, mind. I've got lots more living in me, and I haven't abseiled down a building yet—or swam with sharks.'

'You want to swim with sharks?'

'Great white sharks! The meanest buggers of them all! Oh, aye!'

Mrs Percy's blood pressure was normal. Which

was impressive, seeing as she was talking about one of the greatest predators of all time and being stuck in a tiny cage next to one.

'Well, you're braver than me, Mrs Percy. I'm quite happy to keep my feet on solid ground.'

'Och, that's no way to live, dear. You have to be scared every day. Keeps you fresh. Keeps the blood pumping! You know what I'm talking about, don't you, Dr Brodie? What with your little foray into illness?'

Cameron gave a polite smile and nodded.

'Illness is a mean old beast—we all know that—but it's also the biggest wake-up call.'

'Well, your BP and heart-rate are good. I think as long as you train sensibly and take your time there's no reason why you shouldn't enter the half-marathon if it's really what you want to do.'

'Och, that's brilliant, Doctor. Thank you very much. This your first day, is it?'

Bethan glanced at Cameron and smiled. 'It is. And you're my first patient.'

'Och, really? Do I get a prize?'

'Just the prize of continued good health, Mrs Percy.'

Mrs Percy nodded. 'Aye. 'tis a gift not given to all, but I'm taking full advantage of mine whilst I've got it. How are *you* feeling now, Dr Brodie?'

Cameron's face seemed to flush slightly before he answered, and he wasn't even looking at Bethan. 'Much better, thank you.'

Bethan wondered what Cameron had been ill with. Probably a cold, or something. Maybe the flu? If he was back after a brief illness that might explain the dark circles.

She got up to walk Mrs Percy to the door and held it open for her.

Mrs Percy thanked her. 'Reckon I'll get myself a gold medal one day. Beat the clock.'

'You win if you cross the line at the end, Mrs Percy. That should be your goal. Don't worry about the clock.'

'But the clock's the whole *point*, Doctor. Time's always against us.'

Bethan closed the door and turned to look at Cameron.

He smiled at her casually, guilelessly, as if he had nothing to hide, and she shrugged her worries away.

It had probably just been man-flu.

Nothing to worry about at all.

How many of his patients might give the game away?

That had been a close-run thing with Mrs Percy. She liked to talk…liked to gossip. Oddly, the people who talked non-stop never seemed to come to his surgery with sore throats or laryngitis. But a lot of people in Gilloch knew he'd had a run-in with cancer. They didn't know all the details—he'd only shared those with direct family—but gossip and rumour were rife in a small place such as this.

He'd told everyone else it was over. He'd beaten it. Why upset them? Why put himself in a position of having everyone look at him with sympathy and pity? A dead man walking. They'd be throwing flowers at him before he was six feet under, and who wanted that?

His father had not taken the news of his prognosis well. Why would he? No one wanted to hear things like that. No parent wanted to hear that they would outlive their child, and that was exactly what he'd had to tell his own father.

'They estimate I maybe have a year left.'

He'd almost not told him. The very idea of sitting down in the living room and having to utter those words had made him feel physically sick. He didn't ever want to remind himself of the look on his father's face when he had, silently wiping away his tears, his mouth grim as he looked away and gave one solitary sniff.

'I'm going to leave the practice. I'm going to spend my time with Rosie and you, as much as I can.'

He could appreciate Mrs Percy's outlook on life. You *did* have to grab every second of it. You didn't realise how precious it was until someone told you there wasn't as much left as you thought there was.

Everyone has a limited time. It's just that some have more sand in their hourglass than others.

Bethan sat beside him, typing in the notes about Mrs Percy's consultation, oblivious to his torment and secrets. Her fine fingers were flitting across the keyboard, and he noticed the way she gently bit her lower lip as she concentrated.

She's pretty.

There was no point in telling anyone else the bad news. Sitting down and telling his family had been bad enough—he didn't want to have to keep on repeating it. Seeing people he cared about breaking down and crying and having to be the one to comfort *them*. He needed his strength for himself.

So he'd lied. Told them the chemo had worked. The tumour was gone. It was all over. Life could carry on. Except he'd quite like a year's sabbatical. Just to spend some time with Rosie. It had been a hard few months for her, watching her dad lose his hair and his strength.

Everyone at the practice had understood. They thought it was a marvellous idea, though they'd be sad not to see him every day.

He cleared the dark thoughts from his head. He didn't need to linger on the thought of everyone else's pain. He had a new mantra—*make it all about Rosie.* He wasn't being mean. He wasn't being selfish. But he needed to create distance from people now. They were all too close, all too friendly. He knew what it felt like to lose someone close, and it was horrible. Best to make it easier for everyone by being a little standoffish.

He liked what he'd seen of Bethan so far and she'd been right. But she did exude warmth and an easy-going nature, and he had no doubt he would have a problem keeping her away if she knew the truth. Bethan's ease at being able to chat with her patient as if she'd known her for a long time took skill. If she found out about his glioma he just knew she wouldn't let it go.

And hadn't she been through this before? With her husband? What kind of cruel person would put someone as nice as her through that again?

He hated lying, but he needed to. It was self-preservation.

Cameron thought of all those people in his waiting room—all those familiar faces, all those people he had come to care for. People who would still be here after his time had come and gone.

Part of him didn't want to go. Part of him was still rebelling at his diagnosis—*physician, heal thyself*—and part of him just wanted to lie down and have it all be done with.

He knew that was the depressive side of things. He had tablets for that. For the depression. His consultant had said they would help him come to terms with it. Be less of a shock to the system.

He wasn't sure they were working. He spent far more time than he should wallowing in dark thoughts.

But who wouldn't with a terminal diagnosis?

And why put other people through it when they didn't have to?

It was best to just go quietly.

Let them sort it out after he was gone.

Her first morning of seeing patients was the usual kind of mix. Some were simply curious. Some turned up to see her about some spurious sore throat or trifling cough, just so they could go home and tell everyone else that they'd met Mhairi's prodigal granddaughter.

She treated housemaid's knee, an actual chest infection that needed antibiotics, a suspected urine infection and a clear case of pompholyx—

which was an itchy, painful rash that appeared on the hands and feet. She examined two men complaining of bad backs—one with a shoulder injury after a fall in the garden onto a wooden picnic bench—and diagnosed a case of cellulitis.

She was enjoying herself immensely. Back in the job she loved. Seeing new people—people who would come to mean a lot to her.

She felt Cam's presence behind her like a guardian angel, and he was being as good as his word, letting her be autonomous and get on with everything herself, only butting in when he had to—when there was something she wasn't sure of on the computer, or to tell her where various equipment was stored in the consulting room.

At lunchtime, they stopped for something to eat.

'Well, I think that was a successful morning!' she said, smiling, happy at what she'd achieved. Happy at having been able to help people.

It had been so long since she'd had the experience of feeling she was actually *curing* someone instead of just obscuring their pain. She felt as if she was exactly where she needed to be.

'Aye. You did well,' Cameron said, before gathering up his jacket and bits and pieces.

Bethan followed him through to the staffroom. It wasn't overly large. They were, after all, a small community with a tiny doctor surgery, but it was enough for everyone there. Cosy, comfortable. Apart from Janet, there was an office manager and two nurses. It was enough.

Someone had made a cake—coffee and walnut—and they each took a small slice.

'So, how are you finding it, Doctor?' asked Sarah, the senior nurse.

'It's been good, thank you. Everyone's been so nice. And it's good to feel useful again. Like I'm actually *doing* something. It's great being a mum and staying at home, but after years of watching children's television I was really beginning to feel like my brain was turning into mush.'

There was an odd silence then, and she wasn't sure why. The staff seemed to look at Cameron, then at each other, before looking away and suddenly finding their cake extremely interesting, or sipping from a mug of tea.

What had she said? Was it what she'd said about

staying at home to be a parent? Did they think she was implying that it wouldn't be good for Cameron to do it? That he'd somehow stagnate at being at home? Perhaps they didn't agree with his choice to leave them?

Okay. Tough crowd. But loyal to their boss, which I guess is nice.

'You're from Cornwall—is that right?' asked Sarah, changing the subject.

Bethan smiled, thankful to the nurse for breaking the weird, awkward silence. 'Yes, but I was born here in Gilloch. We moved away when I was a child.'

'What's it like to return home?'

It was odd. Because she hadn't been able to return with her parents. They'd passed away just before her husband had. Being dealt three deaths in quick succession had almost destroyed her. But she'd had to remain strong after her parents had died because Ashley had been sick and deteriorating fast. He'd needed her, needed her strength. She wasn't sure she'd ever grieved properly for her mum and dad. And then there'd been Grace to look after, too.

She'd become a 'coper' because there'd been no other way to be. These last few years it had been like living on autopilot—locked into her routine with Grace each day, because routine was secure and familiar. It made her feel safe. But then, when her grandmother Mhairi had got in touch, she'd realised just how lonely her grandmother was. Nanna had lost her only son, and Bethan and Grace were all she had left.

That yearning for family had increased with every passing day, so Bethan had sold her home in St Austell and moved back to live in Gilloch just a few short months ago. She hadn't resented doing so. Hadn't resented being needed again. It had been so good to see Nanna and Grace's relationship flourish. And she hadn't realised just how much she'd missed having someone love her back. Someone watching out for *her.*

'It's good to be back with family. You never know how long you have left with someone, do you?'

'No.' Sarah smiled at her and bit into her cake.

Being reminded of family made her think of Nanna. She'd no doubt be busy dyeing her wool, but she would be worrying about Bethan's first day at work and would probably appreciate an update.

'Excuse me—I need to make a phone call.' She put down her cake and grabbed her mobile from her handbag, then headed outside.

As she stood outside the surgery, shivering slightly in the cool breeze, she found a bright smile filling her face. She was pleased with how well everything was going. Cameron Brodie was not the tyrant her grandmother believed. In fact he was quite polite. Reserved... Kept his distance...

Smelt great...

'Hey, it's me.'

'Hello, my lovely, how's your first day going?'

Mhairi sounded genuinely interested. Also concerned and fretful. Here, at last, was someone who was worried about *her* feelings.

'It's good.'

'Really? Och, I'm so pleased for you.'

'How's Ye Olde Dyeworks?' That was the name of Nanna's wool business.

'I'm up to my armpits in aubergine and turquoise dye, but it's coming out well. What about you? Had to lance any boils today?'

'No, not yet. They're probably saving that for procedure day. They don't want to scare me off too soon.'

'Well, of course they don't. I was thinking of making your old favourite—custard tarts—for dessert tonight. Fancy that?'

Bethan smiled, remembering the small round tarts her nanna had made for her when she was a little girl. Sprinkled with nutmeg and melting in the mouth with soft, buttery pastry.

'I haven't had those since I was little. They sound great. Thank you.'

'Anything for you, lassie.'

'I'd do anything for *you*, too.'

Cameron helped clear up the lunch mess, put a cover over the rest of the cake and then headed back to his room to await afternoon surgery.

He was surprised to see Bethan already there. 'I didn't know you'd come back in. Have you had time to eat?'

'I'm not that hungry. Running on adrenaline.'

He wanted to make a comment about her looking after herself better, but held it in. She wasn't his concern. He had his own health to worry about. But he felt awkward enough to say *something.*

'Everything all right?'

She smiled brightly. 'Of course!'

'Good. I'm glad to hear that.'

His mind raced to think about who she might have called. Mhairi? Her daughter's school?

'Gilloch Infants' School is very good.'

She seemed puzzled by his comment, so he guessed she hadn't called the school, after all.

'Yes, it seemed to be when we did the tour.'

He nodded, studying her. Then he looked away. She was one of those beautiful women men couldn't help but stare at. But she was *so* beautiful it was difficult to tear his eyes away. He could easily get lost in the soft curves of her face. Her lips, her cheekbones, the downward slope of her nose. The way her hair fell in waves.

Everything about her said *soft.*

His headache began to return—probably because he was allowing himself to become irritated by the track of his thought-processes.

She looks soft, but she had to be strong, right?

She'd nursed her husband through terminal cancer. This was a new start in her life. A new chapter. She looked capable, bright and optimistic. Where had she found that strength?

She told me in her interview that she gets attached quickly, that she gets emotional, but that to her it's a strength, not a weakness.

Perhaps she turned *all* her supposed weaknesses into strengths? Put a positive spin on everything?

He knew it would be best if he just oversaw these next two weeks and then slipped away quietly to live the rest of his life with Rosie. That was what he wanted now. An uncomplicated life. Living with his daughter and bringing her joy whilst he still could. That was who should be his focus. *Rosie.* Not Bethan.

'Ready for the afternoon?' he asked.

She nodded, her eyes bright and gleaming. 'I am!'

Her beauty struck him again. How noble-looking

she was. Even though she'd been through some terrible times, had lost her parents and her husband, she still managed to emit kindness and positivity.

Cam looked out through the window, seeing the heather-covered hills behind the surgery, the dark mountains beyond those. In the slightly grey sky he saw birds circling, their wings buffeted by the wind. Life was beautiful. He should take a page out of Bethan's book and remain optimistic. See the good stuff in life rather than focusing on the bad.

The headaches weren't too bad right now—the painkillers controlled them—and he was able to sleep. The tumour hadn't yet encroached into his optic nerve, so he still had time to *see* that beauty. To remember it for when the time came that his sight was taken from him towards the end.

He sat in his chair as the next patient came in. Caitriona MacDonald. She'd been born deaf and had learnt how to lip-read.

He sat back and observed Bethan checking out Caitriona. She did everything he would have done. She was thorough, and caring, and once again it made him see that even though she had been his only candidate for the post Bethan was absolutely the one he would have chosen even if there'd been a choice of hundreds.

She *was* a people person and, yes, everyone did matter to her. She wanted to do her very best for everyone she saw. Leaving no stone unturned, she checked everything she needed to. There was no slacking. No shortcuts. She did it all.

He felt a sudden need to tell her everything. To just blurt it all out.

To have her look at me like that—the way she's looking and listening to Caitriona.

But then she'd treat him as a patient, wouldn't she? And he didn't want to be the weak one here.

He shifted in his seat, suddenly uncomfortable.

He didn't want her to care for him as he slowly deteriorated. He didn't want her to feel that she was failing again—because doctors always hoped to cheat death if they could.

She'd had enough death in her short life, and she had real patients to care for. Patients who could be cured. Let her concentrate all her efforts on them. She could actually *do* something for them.

Bethan was concluding that Caitriona might have an inner ear infection, and she prescribed some antibiotics and got a promise that Caitriona would return in three weeks to let her know how she'd got on.

They waved their patient goodbye and he watched, fascinated, as Bethan inputted her notes and observations. Her head was bent over the keyboard, her brow furrowed in concentration, her lips gently parted as she bit her bottom lip.

He smiled at the already familiar gesture and felt a pang. Of something. As he looked at her, studied her whilst he could, he realised something else that was disturbing.

I'm attracted to her.

The thought made him smile. He almost chuckled.

The human body was an amazing thing.

The laws of attraction never stopped working. Not until the heart itself ceased beating.

CHAPTER THREE

CAMERON LEFT FOR home exhausted. He'd had no idea just how tiring it was to sit in a chair all day and do nothing except observe someone. And, because he knew how specifically aware he was to Bethan's presence, he'd been determined not to observe her *too* closely. Noticing her beautiful eyes and her smile was *not* the kind of observation he wanted to make.

He was glad to make it to the end of the day and go and collect Rosie from her after-school club. His daughter brought joy into his heart every time he saw her, and renewed his strength and determination.

'How was school?'

'Great! I played with my new friend Grace today.'

Bethan's daughter.

'Really?'

'And, look—I made a caterpillar!'

She ran to fetch her creation from the Art Corner. She had indeed made a caterpillar, from the remains of green cardboard egg cartons, stuck together in a line and painted garish colours.

'Wow! That's fabulous!'

'We're learning about bugs.'

'I can see that.'

'Not the bugs that you have to heal people from.'

He smiled. 'Ah...'

They went home and he made her some dinner. And once she'd had a bath he settled into his favourite part of the day with his daughter. Storytime.

There was nothing he loved more than being able to sit and read with her, making up silly voices and discussing the characters and what they thought was going to happen. Rosie never ceased to amaze him with the insight she had for such a young girl. And his time with her was precious.

How many more stories would he get to read for her? Would they even finish this long book?

What if the tumour damaged his optic nerve soon and he could no longer read? Would she sit upstairs alone? Trying to read by herself?

She'll be alone someday.

That thought almost did him in daily. Rosie was so young. She'd already lost her mother, and now she was going to lose her father, too. Life wasn't fair. But he knew he couldn't allow himself to get lost in the injustice of it all. That way madness lay. His time was short—he couldn't waste it on self-pity. It wasn't how he wanted his daughter to remember him.

He knew that at some point he would have to start letting her stay with his father a bit more, in preparation for when she'd have to live there permanently—after he was gone.

His dad was already trying to make up a room for her to stay in. His old bedroom was being converted from his father's home office. The walls had recently been stripped of the old blue wallpaper and Rosie had picked out a pretty peaches-and-cream pattern she wanted.

He wasn't sure that Rosie understood what was going to happen eventually. Talking to his child about his death was impossible. How much could she truly understand? And was it right to burden her in advance? Instead he'd pretended that he was going to 'go away'. They were trying to make the transition as easy for her as they could, making her new room at his father's a fun thing.

He pointed at the book they were reading. 'You know how in the story Harry lives with his aunt and uncle?'

Rosie nodded.

'Because his own parents aren't around any more?'

Another nod. 'They're dead,' said Rosie.

'Well, you'll be doing that one day. Living with Grandpa Doug?'

She seemed to think about it. 'But I won't be in the cupboard under the stairs, will I? I'm having my own room.'

'That's right.' He smiled.

'And Grandpa Doug is *nice* to me. Not like Harry's family.'

'Grandpa Doug is *very* nice. And he loves you loads.'

'And you'll be gone away?'

He swallowed hard. 'That's right. I won't be able to come back, but you'll be able to see me in here.' He touched the side of her head. 'And in here.' He pointed at where her heart was.

Rosie seemed to think about this for a while. Then, 'Who'll read to me at night?'

'Grandpa Doug will.'

'But he doesn't do the voices.'

Cameron kissed the top of her head and smiled to himself, loving it that her greatest concern was the right voices for her story. If that was her greatest worry, then it would be fine. He was happy with that. He could carry all the other worries by himself.

That was how it should be anyway. She was too young to be burdened by the world. And he didn't want to tell his daughter he was going to die. How could he?

'Right—hush, now. One more chapter and then it's sleepy time, okay?'

'Okay, Daddy.'

And she snuggled into his side and listened until she fell fast asleep.

* * *

It was raining, and the roads were slick with water and puddles. Beneath the endless grey sky Bethan parked her car, right outside the surgery door, ready to do a day of home visits after she'd collected the medical files and any equipment she might need.

She liked it that the practice had a whole day to do home visits. Not every practice offered this service any more, but she'd always enjoyed doing them. You didn't always get to understand a person's home-life and true situation from an eight-minute consultation in the surgery, so it was good to see people in their own environment. And there were quite a few people who couldn't get to the surgery, so it was a worthwhile opportunity for them all.

She merrily chirped a hello to Janet on Reception.

'Good morning, Dr Monroe! How are you today?'

'Good, thank you. How are you?'

'Bonny, Doctor, always bonny.'

She smiled and passed on through to the office to collect her schedule.

Cameron was already there, checking the files off against a list. He looked up when he saw her and she was struck by how pale he looked today. He was pale anyway—the standard complexion for someone with such beautiful red hair—but today that paleness had an ashen quality to it. And the shadows beneath his eyes looked darker than they had before.

Had he had a bad night's sleep? Was he still recovering from that bout of flu?

'Morning, Dr Brodie.'

'Cam, please.' He smiled. 'We've got time for a brief cuppa before we head out. Can I make you one?'

'Oh, thank you. That would be lovely.'

She'd managed to make a cup of tea first thing that morning, but she'd only had a couple of sips, in her rush to get Grace ready for school, and then her nanna had asked her to help bring down some wool skeins from the spare room she used as a dye room—she needed to get them off in the post. She'd spent so much time running around her tea had gone cold and there hadn't been time to make a fresh one.

She sighed with delight as he passed her a hot, steaming mug. 'Perfect.'

'We've got twelve house calls to make today—which doesn't sound much, but a lot of these patients can talk for ever, so we'll need to keep an eye on the time.'

'All right. Anything in particular I should know about?'

He raised an eyebrow and looked uncomfortable. 'Well, one of the patients is my grandfather, Angus Brodie. He can be a bit of a...a curmudgeon.'

His grandfather? The infamous Angus?

'Okay.'

'He can get a bit...grumpy.'

Cam was looking as if 'grumpy' was the most polite word he could come up with for his grandfather, so she smiled in sympathy. Did Angus know who she was? Mhairi's granddaughter? Would he be biased against her, the way Nanna was against him?

Cam looked exhausted. Was he fit to do a full day of home visits?

'And are you okay? You look a little…washed out.'

He stared right back at her, his face set in a stern frown that brooked no argument. 'I'm bonny.'

Yes, you look it, she thought with wry amusement. Clearly he was not a man who admitted weakness.

He was a good man. A strong man. Handsome, too. But she was trying her best not to notice *that* part.

She'd spoken to Nanna about him the previous night.

'He was very sweet all day.'

'He can afford to be. He's your boss.'

'It wasn't like that, Nanna. He was charming and considerate and kind.'

'Easy on the eye, too, I bet? Don't you blush like that, young Bethan. I've seen him.'

'He's a widower, Nanna. And devoted to his daughter. I don't think he's looking for love.'

'*All* men look for love—at least until they nail down the coffin lid.'

Bethan had gone to bed that night understanding why the young women of Gilloch might all look twice at Cameron Brodie. Why wouldn't they? *She* had. All day. Stealing looks when she'd thought he wouldn't see. He was handsome, tall, rugged and broad, clearly intelligent and a dedicated father. Who *wouldn't* want to be noticed and cared for by a man like that?

It had made her think about her own love-life as she'd lain in bed alone. She hadn't given it much thought after Ashley died. She'd been concentrating on Grace. Getting them both through. Getting them through the trauma and out the other side in one piece. Men had not been on her radar because she'd given her all to Ashley—especially in those last few weeks. It had been all she'd thought about—getting through each day. She'd not given any thought to dating again. Not back then.

But now…?

Cameron Brodie was hot, no doubt about it, but they'd both had loss in their lives and that did something to a person. It marked them. Sometimes it made people afraid to talk to you, as if they didn't quite know what to say. It was a lonely experience, but it was one that united them. They'd both lost a spouse. They were both single parents with girls the same age. She felt a connection to him. An understanding. She might be on the lookout for romance, but would she find it with a colleague?

'You must be looking forward to the time you're going to have with Rosie. No more long days spent at work or rushing out in the middle of the night on call!'

He settled into the chair opposite her, looking rugged in dark jeans and a red plaid shirt. He looked as if he was going to go and chop some wood.

'I am. But I'll miss this, too. My job. All my life I wanted to be a doctor. Never changed my mind once. And yet here I am—giving it up.'

'But only for a year!' She smiled, trying to imply that a year wasn't that long and he'd be back before he knew it. 'When you come back you'll be raring to go again.'

He nodded. Looked away. Sipped his tea. 'Sure.'

Bethan frowned. There seemed to be something more to this situation, but he clearly wasn't going to tell her about it. And why would he?

Cam got up out of his chair and started packing the items they might need. Clearly, for him, the subject was closed, and she was puzzled by the abrupt change from polite conversation to something that had touched a nerve.

What am I not seeing? Or perhaps I am seeing it, but not understanding it?

He was pale. And those shadows beneath his eyes...

Was he suffering from stress? Being a GP *could* be incredibly stressful—listening to people complaining all day about their ailments, bringing you their problems for you to solve. It heaped a whole lot of responsibility on a doctor's shoulders and not everyone could bear that easily.

She watched him pack, his large, capable hands, quickly gathering all the equipment, methodical as he ticked off a checklist, clearly back in the world of work and not listening to probing questions.

Perhaps it was best if she gave him his personal space. Clearly he didn't want her asking anything more, and she had only known him a day. It wasn't her place. Not yet.

There's still time to find out. We have nine more days of working together.

But she couldn't help but worry about him. She packed her own medical kit, stealing glances at him as he worked. She frowned.

Had the loss of his wife changed him?

Losing Ashley had deeply affected *her*.

She followed him out of the room, out of the surgery and to her car. She pressed the key fob, allowing him into the passenger side, and decided that at the end of the day, when their list was over, she would offer him a listening ear.

Perhaps all he needed was a friend who understood?

The first patient on their list was a Mrs Cromarty. Seventy-nine years old and unable to get around much because of a bad case of cellulitis in her left leg and an open wound on her foot that never seemed to heal properly. Mrs Cromarty had apparently developed the infection after a fall in her back garden, when she'd tripped over a crooked paving slab as she tended to her runner beans.

Bethan parked outside an old stone cottage that sat in a small terrace of four and grabbed her bag from the back seat. She rapped her knuckles on the front door, which was painted a pale duck-egg-blue, and smiled when she saw a small sign that said, *Only come knocking when this place ain't a rocking.*

Cam smiled at her reaction. 'Mrs Cromarty has a delicious sense of humour—despite her situation.'

It took some time for Mrs Cromarty to make it to the door, and when she did Bethan was confronted by a tiny woman who couldn't be more than five feet tall, walking with the aid of a stick.

'You must be the new doctor?' She peered around Bethan. 'Hello, Dr Brodie.'

'Morning, Vera, how are you today?' he asked.

'Still alive, so I can't complain.'

They followed Vera Cromarty—very slowly—back into her living room. It was a cosy room, with crocheted blankets draped over chairs and pristine white antimacassars on the arms for extra protection. Every conceivable surface was filled with little knick-knacks—mostly small animals—and in the middle of the sofa, curled into a tight ball, was a very large, very fat, ginger cat.

'Don't mind Moriarty. He won't mind you.' Vera settled back into a chair with a heavy sigh, slightly out of breath. 'I'd offer you tea, but it takes me so long to walk it'd be cold by the time you got it.'

'Don't worry, Mrs Cromarty, we had tea just before we left. Now, how are you today?'

'Not bad, Doctor, not bad. Can't complain.'

Bethan raised an eyebrow. 'But if you *were* to complain, what would you say?'

Vera sighed. 'Well, the leg is slowing me down, I can't move it much because it's swollen so badly. It means all my friends have to come here to see me and I don't get out. Your grandmother was here just the other day. She's a lovely woman, Mhairi. Very kind.'

Bethan smiled. So Nanna and Vera Cromarty were friends…

'She was so excited you were coming back to live with her here in Gilloch. She's been terribly lonely…so alone since she lost your grandad…and then when your poor father died, too…' Vera crossed herself. 'She had nobody. Absolutely nobody! I thought she'd die of a broken heart—I really did, poor wee thing. But look at you now—all grown up! I remember when you were a wee bairn. You were just the sweetest thing. Not that you aren't now, of course. You're beautiful! You've got your father's eyes and—' She suddenly seemed to remember something. 'I'm *so* sorry. You lost your husband, didn't you? Just terrible! *Terrible!*'

Bethan looked briefly at Cam and smiled.

'Cancer, wasn't it? You must have had an awful time. Thank the Lord that you had your own wee bairn to get you through. Grace, isn't it? Do you have a picture?'

'Er…not on me, no.' She did have a picture. It was in her purse. But she didn't feel it was appropriate to share personal details with a patient. Even if that patient already seemed to know so much about her.

'I lost my Seamus to cancer. Brutal disease. *Brutal!*'

Out of the corner of her eye she saw Cam check his watch. He looked a little antsy.

'He had it in his lungs… Mind you, he'd been a smoker all his life, so we shouldn't have been surprised, but there was no dignity in it. None at all. He suffered at the end—he truly did. If I could have put him out of his misery, then I would have done, God rest his soul. I know we shouldn't say things like that, but it's the honest truth. We wouldn't let dogs suffer the way they let my Seamus suffer. If he'd have been a wee terrier the vet would have put him down. Dr Brodie here prescribed morphine for him, but it was never enough.' She wiped her eyes and sniffed. 'Never enough…'

Bethan stared at Vera Cromarty, not sure what to say. There had been some tough days with Ashley. Days when he'd seemed in so much pain and the Oramorph had barely touched it. Days when she'd become frustrated with her own skills as a doctor, unsure of what she could do to help him.

But there'd also been days when she'd sat by his bedside, holding his hand, and they'd just talked.

Talked about everything. Silly stuff. Deep and meaningful stuff. Those were the moments she treasured. Laughing with him. Reminiscing. Remembering the good times. It had been a long time since they'd just sat together and talked. They'd always been so busy, before, both of them...

'I'm sorry for your loss, Mrs Cromarty.'

'Vera, pet.'

Bethan nodded, mindful of the time. 'Vera. Well, let me check you out, see how that wound's getting along. Are you still taking your antibiotics?'

She'd run out, she said, but when Bethan unwrapped the leg and saw that the wound still looked as if it wasn't healing, she wondered if Vera was on the *correct* antibiotics?

She checked her patient's file, to see what she'd been given so far, and saw they'd been pretty broad-spectrum.

'I'm going to take a swab of the wound, Vera. See if we can culture whatever it is that's keeping it open and get you some focused medication.'

'And that should make it better, should it?'

'Hopefully, yes.'

Bethan redressed the wound, and all the time Vera chatted non-stop about how Bethan had once played in Vera's front garden, and how she had come in with mud all over her face, having tried to eat a mud pie.

She laughed so much, trying to describe the look on the face of Bethan's mum, that Bethan was soon laughing, too, at her childhood antics.

It seemed that Vera had an endless supply of stories, and Cam eventually interrupted her by standing up. 'I'm sorry, Vera, but we must go.'

Bethan was surprised by his terse manner, but chose not to say anything. He was still technically her boss, and he *had* told her that some of their patients could talk for Scotland.

Vera nodded solemnly, clearly sad to be losing her audience. 'You tell that grandmother of yours I've got that book she was after. She can come round anytime to get it.'

'I will. Thank you. Now, you take care of yourself, and I'll call you when the results of the swab come in.'

'All right, pet. We'll speak again soon.'

'Don't get up. We'll see ourselves out.'

Bethan and Cam hurried outside, back to the car, keen to get on their way.

'I never thought we'd get away,' Cam said, sounding irritated.

'She's probably lonely if she's not getting out much.'

'Believe you me—Vera Cromarty could talk your ears off *before* she got housebound.'

Bethan smiled. 'Where to next?'

'Wide Way Farm. It's on the outskirts of the village.'

'Direct me?' She started the engine and began to drive.

There was silence in the car for a while, almost as if they were both enjoying the rest their ears were receiving, and then Cameron broke it to ask her a surprising question.

'How does Grace cope without her father?'

A flurry of thoughts and emotions swirled around her for a moment in a blizzard of uncertainty. Uncomfortably so.

She kept her gaze on the road ahead as she answered, surprised that he'd asked. 'She was a baby when he died. She never really knew him. I don't think she has any memories, and if she does it's because of the stories I've told her about him.'

He seemed to think about this. 'But she's happy?'

That question was easier. 'Yes, she is. I'm sure it will get a little more difficult when she's older. Perhaps when she's a teenager?' A thought occurred to her. 'You must have similar concerns? Because Rosie doesn't have a mother? Are you worried about her not having a maternal influence?'

He looked out of the window, away across the open fields to the gentle hues of heather and gorse, greens and purples and greys, that swept away from them off to the horizon. There was a brown partridge pecking at the ground that held his attention for a moment.

'A little.' He sounded gruff.

'Children are very resilient. We have to give them more credit.'

He didn't say anything.

'But you wouldn't be a good parent if you didn't worry. I think it's part of the job description.'

'Take the next right here.' He pointed to an up-coming lane.

She gave him a quick sideways glance. Some of his colour had returned. He looked a lot health-ier than he had done this morning. But clearly he had things on his mind.

'Things get better when you get a decent night's sleep,' she said.

He turned to look at her. 'What makes you think I'm not sleeping?'

'Well, no offence, but you look like you haven't had a decent night's sleep in weeks. Have you been worrying about things? Giving up work? The changes that are coming? I can imagine it's very stressful.'

She could sense him staring at her. Consider-ing her. She gave him a quick smile—one that she hoped conveyed friendship and not interfer-ence. She was a doctor. She couldn't help but no-tice the signs that his body was under stress and that he was trying to power through whatever was ailing him.

'I'm fine.'

And even though it was clear he didn't want

to discuss it, she couldn't help babbling. 'It's intense, being a single parent. We have no one to share our worries and fears with, so we end up all alone with our thoughts and we carry those concerns like burdens. Sometimes we have to let go of them—even if it's just for half an hour. Have you tried doing something to reduce stress? Yoga, perhaps? Or meditation?'

She knew a lot of people who swore by these solutions. Taking some time out to just breathe and concentrate on the body and relaxation. Sometimes it could be enough to make things bearable.

Cameron laughed, but it wasn't a pleasant sound. It seemed bitter.

'Yoga? I think I'm past the point of needing the Downward Dog as a cure-all.'

'A *real* dog, then? Pets are known as great stress-relievers! Unless you already have one, of course?'

She glanced at him, saw his brow was lined with a deep frown, and suddenly wondered if she was overstepping the mark. Getting into his personal business. Trying to fix him when he was a doctor himself. And weren't medics the worst kind of patient?

'I'm sorry, Cam. This is none of my business.'

'You're right. It's not.'

I've upset him.

She wanted him to leave the practice knowing he had left it in the most capable hands. She wanted him to feel good. She *cared*. He was a fellow single parent in the trenches, for one thing!

The lane they were on took them through a gorgeous tree tunnel. It was as if Mother Nature was trying to embrace them as they drove through, and when they emerged on the other side she spotted a lone farmhouse, surrounded by flocks of woolly sheep.

'Is that Wide Way?'

'Mmm. Just follow the road and then take the left-hand turning when it comes up. And watch out for Robbie.'

'Robbie?'

'The sheepdog. He's often roaming the grounds.'

'All right... You know this patient well?'

He sighed. 'I should do. This is my grandfather's farm.'

A sense of foreboding went through her. Anticipation? Fear? She'd heard many tales about Angus Brodie. He was a formidable man, by all accounts. True, most of her knowledge about him came from her grandmother, but...

Never trust a Brodie.

And here she sat. Beside one whom she liked and respected and about to treat one she hadn't met, but who was causing her great anticipation.

Nanna had said the man had ruined her life and reputation. Cam had said he was a grumpy curmudgeon. Would he be as terrible as everyone made out?

Her hands trembled slightly as she turned into the farm's long driveway, and she hoped that Cameron didn't notice as her car rumbled along the pitted and potholed drive. She saw no dog running loose, which was good, because she didn't think they'd get off to a good start if she ran over the family sheepdog.

'What am I seeing him for?'

She should have asked earlier. If she had then she would have had time to consider everything she knew about his condition.

She wanted to walk into Wide Way Farm as a solid professional with whom Angus Brodie would find no fault. He would think of her as a good, friendly doctor whom he could trust.

He was her patient now. Not just her nanna's ex-beau. Best to set the tone for the rest of their relationship on a positive footing.

'He's developed a rash. Told me he thinks it's shingles.'

'You haven't seen him yourself?'

'No. He only rang me last night, so I made him an appointment. I told him he'd be seeing you. It's not good to treat your own family. He...er... wasn't too impressed when he found out who you were.'

'Right.'

She pulled the car to a stop and just sat there for a moment to steady her breathing. To try and calm herself so that she could present the illusion of being a professional who was in control.

'You okay?' Cam was looking at her.

'Fine!' She tried to sound breezy, but she'd have been lying if she hadn't admitted she was nervous.

All the stories she'd heard about Angus Brodie but she'd never met him. And now here she was. Quaking in her boots. Trying to seem brave. If he'd already taken against her, he might be a difficult patient.

'We…er…we'd better go inside. He doesn't like to be kept waiting.'

The farmhouse door opened and a round woman with a huge bosom and wiry grey hair tied back in a low bun emerged, her arms open in greeting.

This was it. The lion's den.

She was trying to joke away her fear, but it was real and palpable. Nanna had made this man out to be the devil himself.

Swallowing hard, she opened the car door, her legs trembling as she grabbed her doctor's bag from the back seat. A border collie was suddenly sniffing at her trouser legs, and she held out her hand for it to sniff. The dog licked her fingertips and then ran away to smell something else.

She stood up, straightening her spine, trying to find the courage inside that she knew she'd need to get her through the next few minutes. She did have it inside her. She had got through the deaths of her parents and the death of her husband, she was raising a child alone and she was doing a great job!

Buoyed up, she walked with determination across to where Cameron stood with the woman who could only be his grandmother.

'Mrs Brodie? Dr Bethan Monroe.' She held out her hand for the woman to shake.

Cam's grandmother beamed a smile at her. 'Hello, lass. He's in the bedroom. Hasn't got up today. I guess I ought to take you through.'

'Lead the way.'

Bethan swallowed a very tiny amount of saliva as she followed Cam and his grandmother up the stairs.

At least she's *friendly!*

Cam's grandmother led them into a large bedroom, and the first thing Bethan saw was a beautiful bedspread in shades of purple. It looked hand-quilted and stitched. And there, at the head of the bed, propped up by a vast mountain of pillows, sat an old man, with a balding pate and a white beard. Circular reading glasses were perched on the end of his nose.

'Cameron!' Angus looked pleased to see his grandson. A broad smile broke across his face, but it quickly disappeared as Bethan appeared from behind him.

Cam's grandfather looked startled. Then angry. His eyes darkened and a withered hand pointed at her. '*You...* You're the new doctor?'

She smiled, determined to make him like her. 'Yes, I—'

'You ought to be ashamed of yourself! How *dare* you come to my house? How dare you walk in here, bold as you like, treading in a dead man's shoes!'

Wait? What?

Angus pointed at Cam emphatically. 'He is *dying*! Dying! And you think you can replace him? Get out of here. I don't want to see you. *Get out!*' he raged, his voice a throaty roar.

Bethan was confused as she stared at the angry old man in the bed. His face was red with fury and rage, and Cam was doing his best to calm the old man down, but the most puzzling thing was the words that were swirling around in her brain.

'He is dying! And you think you can replace him?'

Who was dying?

The only person she was replacing was Cam, and that was just for a year...

Her eyes met Cam's and instantly she knew the truth. In his blue eyes she saw the reality of his situation. The guilt. The admission as he looked down and away.

Cam had been sick. She knew that.

But clearly whatever it was that ailed him had not gone away.

He was not going on a year's sabbatical.

He was going to die.

And he'd lied to everyone.

Including her.

She swallowed back her tears and squared her shoulders.

Bethan looked pale and shaken, but somehow she steadied her voice and met the senior Brodie's eyes.

'Mr Brodie,' she began. 'I am your doctor and you have an appointment. I am here to help you. Now, if you *do* have shingles, and you want to get better, I need to examine your rash and decide on an appropriate treatment regime.'

Her chin lifted. Clearly she was determined to stare him down if necessary.

Her courage, her bravery, astounded Cam. And it made him like her even more than he already did. No one had ever stood up against his grandfather like this. The grumpy old man had a temper bad enough to scare off rabid dogs.

And now she knows about me.

He looked down at the floor as he sucked in a breath of his own. She was persistent. She was strong. She was not the type of person to let this news go without a fight. And it irked him that he was going to have to let her get involved.

Angus stared back at her, clearly taken aback that she was not going to be cowed by him. There was a pregnant pause, an atmosphere so thick nobody could move. They all stood like statues, waiting for Angus Brodie's approval.

The old man curled his lip and looked away. 'Do what you have to.'

Cam looked at Bethan.

A small smile of triumph powered her forward to stand by his grandfather's bed.

'Okay. Let's see what we can do for you.'

CHAPTER FOUR

SHE STEPPED TOWARDS his bed. 'May I sit down?'

He looked at the chair beside his bed. 'Suit yourself.'

She pulled it closer and looked him square in the face. Her heart was racing like mad, and she felt sure there were rivulets of sweat running down her back and beneath her arms, but she forged onwards anyway.

It had taken a lot to stand up to him, but she was damned if he was going to intimidate her. She was not of her grandmother's generation. Women did not have to be cowed by patriarchal men any more.

He's dying. Cam's dying.

Her brain wanted to focus on that. The thought kept echoing around her skull. But she couldn't give it any time right now. She had to concentrate on Angus and treat him. Cameron's health would have to be touched upon later. Maybe when they were back in the car, or after they'd finished the home visits. People were depending on them to see them. To keep it together and not be distracted.

But what could it be? What was wrong with him?

Don't be cancer. Please, don't let it be cancer.

'You have a rash? Would you like to show me where?'

Angus glared at her, but slowly began to unbutton his pyjama top, opening it to reveal an angry red, blistering rash that curved under his chest and slightly around to his back, beneath his right shoulder blade. It looked very sore and painful.

'It does look like shingles. How long have you had it?'

'A couple of days.'

She nodded and reached into her bag for a prescription pad. 'I'll write you up for some acyclovir. It won't kill the virus, but it will help stop it multiplying. You could also take paracetamol for the pain you're experiencing.'

'Right.' Angus redid the buttons on his top.

'Keep the area as clean and dry as you can, and wear loose-fitting tops like the one you have on now.'

She turned to look at Cam's grandmother.

'You can use calamine for any itching, and if any of the blisters begin to weep at all you could use a cool compress—a flannel wrung out with cool water will do. And don't share his towels with anyone else in the house.'

'Yes, Doctor,' she said.

'Anything else?' Angus asked, clearly resentful of her orders.

'If it gets any worse please call the surgery and I'll come out to see you again. See how you're doing. Is there anything else I can help you with whilst I'm here?'

Normally she wouldn't be so curt with a patient. It wasn't her style at all. But she figured that today she would keep it simple and to the point and then, over time, they might expand their trust and friendliness towards each other.

'No. I'm fine. Thank you.'

She nodded and stood up, packing away her things, snapping her bag shut and going to leave the room. In the doorway she stopped, had a thought and turned around.

'I'm a good doctor, Mr Brodie. A good person. But I'm here to be me. I'm not trying to replace anyone.'

He said nothing, so she turned to go down the stairs, but as she went she heard Angus Brodie clear his throat and speak once more.

'You're Mhairi's granddaughter.'

It wasn't a question.

She turned, wondering where this was leading. 'I am.'

He nodded, clearly uncomfortable making conversation with her. 'Your father... Mhairi's son... he's passed away?'

She gave a curt nod, not sure whether or not Angus was about to rain down insults against her dead father. If he was, she was going to stop him in his tracks! She would *not* have her father bad-mouthed.

But he didn't. He simply nodded in understanding, his eyes darkening with sadness. 'You tell her I'm sorry for her loss.' He looked up. 'And for yours.'

Bethan stood there shocked. Sympathy was the *last* thing she would have expected from Angus Brodie!

'Thank you. I'll pass that on.'

She followed Cam and Mrs Brodie down the stairs, still a little on the back foot as to what had just happened. Was that Angus's way of holding out an olive branch? Or was he seeing similarities between himself and Mhairi? Nanna had lost her son and he foresaw himself losing Cam?

They walked outside and congregated by the car.

Cam hugged his grandmother and told her he'd see her soon and Bethan studied him, looking for clues, for signs that he was dying. Could it be true? She'd seen him take painkillers a few times, but he'd always brushed it off as a headache. He was pale… And those dark circles under his eyes—were they a sign?

'I'm leaving to spend time with my daughter.'

Life didn't seem fair. He was a good man. A father. She'd hoped he would be a good friend. For some reason she didn't understand she felt a small sting of tears at the backs of her eyes—

which was weird, because she barely knew him. It had to be because she liked him. Liked him a lot. She'd hoped she was making a new friend, and now she was going to lose him before they could create that friendship.

And, as she'd told him in that interview, which seemed so long ago now, she got attached quickly. She got attached and emotionally involved. She couldn't help it. It was her nature. She cared for her fellow human beings and she'd seen enough suffering in her life already.

Would she have to watch him suffer, too?

And what about Rosie?

If she knew *she* were dying, leaving Grace as an orphan...

Bethan blinked back tears and got inside the car.

As they drove away from Wide Way Farm, Cameron found himself biting down on his lip, not sure what to say.

How could he explain all that Bethan had heard and learnt inside the farmhouse with his grandfather? Was it best to say nothing? To pretend that she'd misheard?

He shook his head, not enjoying the idea of outright lying to her. But he was angry that she was now involved. Of all the people in the world he *didn't* want to lay this on, she was the foremost. Because of what had happened with her husband. She'd already done this. She'd lost someone, and so had he, and he damn well knew how painful that was.

But he wasn't sure what to say. He'd kept her out of it for a day. Just a day! He hadn't known his grandfather would react to her so vehemently.

Now she knew, would she tell everyone else?

'I'd appreciate it if you kept what you've learnt to yourself.'

She kept her eyes on the road, her hands steady on the wheel. 'Well, it falls under patient confidentiality, doesn't it?'

She sounded hurt. Betrayed. But how could that be? They hadn't known each other long. Was it his lying that caused her to sound like that?

'I'm not your patient, but…thank you.'

She continued to drive, her eyes on the road,

not once glancing at him. 'We need to talk about it, though. We can't not. Not now that I know.'

'I know.'

He looked out of the window at the low grey sky, at the dark clouds overhead threatening later rainfall. The sky was grey...the mountains were grey. Even the heathers that were normally so bright and full of colour looked dull today. Muted.

He didn't want to lay any of this at her door, but he knew he would have to tell her the full truth now.

'Why don't you come to my house after work today? Bring Grace. The girls can play and we can talk in another room.'

She was frowning. But she nodded. 'Okay. To-night, then.'

She indicated to take a left turn and let out a long, low breath.

He glanced at her. At the small divot between her dark eyebrows, the determined set of her jaw. This was a woman who would not let him get away with any excuses. She *did* get attached and emotionally involved. Exactly as she'd warned him she would.

Cam pulled up the next patient's file. 'All right. Back to work, then. We're off to number seventeen, Hudson Road. Mrs Davina McClane.'

'Work. Yes. Absolutely.'

But he could tell the atmosphere between them had changed. No longer were they just employer and employee. No longer was it all about two colleagues working together. Now it was about two people who shared a terrible secret. It was a secret that he had no doubt would spread throughout their small community as his condition deteriorated, but for now it was theirs.

Bethan knew about death. About people dying from cancer. She'd lived through it—was a survivor of that war.

He was a soldier, fighting a losing battle.

Knowing that he was not going to win.

Bethan walked through the front door and Grace ran straight into her arms. 'Mummy!'

She scooped up her daughter and squeezed her tight, cherishing the love and comfort that her daughter gave her, inhaling her scent, enjoying the feel of her little body, relishing the moment of holding someone she loved.

Here was a pure relationship. A relationship with no secrets.

It had been a long, difficult day, and the atmosphere in the car had been strained after their visit to Angus Brodie, the friendship that they had only just begun to cultivate, already under strain.

She hoped that when she went to his home later and heard the truth—the full story—they could go back a few steps and start again. But this time from a stronger place, because this time she would know everything. But apprehension and fear filled her heart. She wasn't sure she was ready to hear such a story yet again. Such dreadful news…

'Mummy, I drew a ladybird! Come and look!'

Grace slithered from her arms and ran into the kitchen, from which delicious smells emanated. Slow-cooked beef, if she wasn't mistaken.

'Okay, I'm coming.' She hung up her coat and bag and went into the kitchen to admire her daughter's drawing. Nanna was there, seated at the kitchen table preparing vegetables. 'Hello, Nanna. Something smells nice.'

'Beef hotpot. I'm just about to steam some broccoli and carrots to go with it.' Nanna looked up at her and frowned. 'How was your day? You look done in.'

'It was long.'

She took a moment to tell Grace how beautiful her picture was, stuck to the fridge by a magnet from the Isle of Mull, and then sat down for a moment.

Grace skipped from the room and Bethan turned back to her grandmother. 'I had to see Angus Brodie today.'

Mhairi stiffened and put down her knife. 'Oh. How did that wee delight go?'

Bethan sighed. 'Horribly. He was on our list of home visits.'

'And he let you treat him? Wonders will never cease.' She picked her knife up again and continued to peel carrots.

'He told me something. Something that I…'

The words choked in her throat and she knew she couldn't continue. It was not her secret to tell.

'Something?'

She decided to change the subject. 'He asked after you.'

Mhairi coloured, her lined cheeks flushing a rosy red. 'Me? Whatever for?'

Bethan shrugged. 'He just asked after you. Told me to tell you that he was sorry for the loss of Dad.'

Mhairi got up from the table, deliberately keeping her back to Bethan as she messed around by the kettle, noisily preparing two cups of tea.

'He must have heard about it and he offered his condolences.'

Mhairi slammed shut the cupboard door from which she'd got the mugs. 'Well, it was a few years ago now. He's a bit late.'

Bethan shrugged. 'I'm just passing on the message. I was surprised he even said it—I mean, I didn't think he was meant to care about you.'

'He doesn't. He was probably just being polite because he had to be. Though that would have been a world first for Angus Brodie.'

'He wasn't polite to start with.'

'I bet!'

'He yelled at me.'

Mhairi turned, came back to the table and grabbed Bethan's hand within her own, squeezing it tight. 'Och, that *horrible* man! Are you all right?'

She nodded. 'It was okay. I told him that I was his doctor and he ought to treat me with some respect.'

Mhairi cackled. 'Och, I wish I could have been there to see that!'

Bethan smiled, then looked down at the table. 'I've been invited to Cam's tonight, but we'll eat here before we go.'

Mhairi stared. 'Why do you have to go there?'

'We have some things to discuss about today. Work stuff. I'm going to take Grace to play with Rosie—they're in the same class.'

'Och, I'm not sure I'm comfortable with all this.'

'We're just talking, Nanna. It's not like it's a *date*!'

She laughed, to relieve the tension, but Mhairi didn't laugh with her as she'd expected.

Mhairi just stared at her. 'It had better not be. Be careful, lass.' She laid a hand on hers. 'You can't trust them.'

'It's not like it's a date!'

So why was she upstairs in her bedroom, choosing what clothes to wear when she went to Cam's house?

She'd spent the entire day with him. Working. Tending to patients. All of whom had been delightful with the exception of Angus Brodie. There'd been a few tentative enquiries about her life from one or two others who knew her grandmother, but that had been it.

Some of the patients had wanted to know about her time in Cornwall. About how she'd met Ashley, about Grace, and then the horrible twists of fate that had driven her back to Gilloch, to the only family she had left.

It had made her think about Ashley's parents. About how they must be missing seeing Grace every day. They lived in Cornwall, too. In Polperro—a small fishing village on the south coast.

She'd felt guilty about leaving them behind, knowing she was taking Grace—their one connection to their son. But they'd had the first few years of Grace's life and Nanna had only ever seen her online or talked to her on the phone!

Besides, she'd had to do what she'd felt was right. She was Grace's mother and she would make the decision that was best.

I ought to call them. Maybe send one or two photos so they don't feel out of the loop.

Her wardrobe was open before her. She was *not* choosing fancy clothes to look nice for Cameron.

What did you wear to hear a confession? They were going to be talking. He was going to explain everything. Probably tell her something horrible.

She was choosing different clothes because she'd been working in these all day and she wanted to feel fresh. So she picked out an aquamarine dress and a cropped cream cardigan and lay them on her bed, before taking a shower to wash away the cares of the day. To prepare herself mentally for what lay ahead.

This time she'd got a warning.

As she stood under the spray she thought about what she would be discussing with Cam. His illness. His sickness. What could it be?

She'd been through cancer with Ashley, so she fervently hoped it wasn't that. It was such a cruel disease, and she wasn't sure she could watch someone go through that again. Which she would have to do—as a doctor, if nothing else. She would be the one caring for him, making his days as comfortable as she could.

It could be Huntington's... Motor Neurone Disease?

He was so young! To be struck down in the prime of life and with a small child to worry about...

She felt for him. In one way she'd had it easy, with Grace being a baby. She'd not had to explain to a small child what was happening to her daddy, because Grace had only just been learning to sit up and make tentative attempts to crawl when Ashley had died.

Rosie would *know*. She knew who her father was. She loved him. He was her everything.

Bethan wiped away tears at the thought of being in a similar situation, having to find the words to explain such a thing to Grace.

She wrapped her hair in a towel and went through to her bedroom, to find Nanna standing in the doorway, looking at the dress.

'Everything okay?'

She nodded, then pointed at the dress. 'That's pretty.'

'Oh, thanks. I got it ages ago.'

'It'll bring out the colour of your eyes.'

'Will it? That's not why I'm wearing it,' she said irritably, meeting her nanna's gaze. She didn't want her worrying, but Nanna knew nothing about Cam's news just yet, and she didn't feel right telling her that she was going to Cameron's house to hear about his diagnosis.

'You'll look very pretty. But then, why wouldn't you? You're a beautiful young woman. I'm very proud.'

'Thanks.'

Nanna sank onto the bed. 'Can I ask…when you met Angus today…was he really sick?'

Bethan smiled to herself. Beneath all that bluster, all that hot air, there was still a little nuance of concern for Angus Brodie.

'I can't tell you that, Nanna. Patient confidentiality.'

'Och, I know, but… He's not at death's door, or anything?'

'No. No, he's not.'

Nanna nodded, somewhat mollified. 'Good. That's good. Well, I'll let you get on with it, then. Will you be back late?'

'I shouldn't think so. I'll have Grace back for her bedtime.'

Nanna seemed happy with that, and left Bethan to get dressed.

Cam lived in a very picturesque cottage that she found instantly charming and quaint. It was made of old Highland stone, with a low thatched roof and a pistachio-green door, and the front garden contained a small blue rowing boat that was being used as a garden planter, overflowing with flowers in bright, cerise pinks and rich, heathery purples. By the front door was an old pair of wellington boots that tumbled dark green ivy onto the stepping stone path. It was whimsical, with a nod to the fishing traditions that this village had been made from. She liked it. Could almost imagine herself working in this garden herself.

'Mummy, look—a boat!' said Grace.

'Yes, I see it.'

She walked up to the front door, the nerves in her stomach chasing each other around like children playing tag, and rapped the lion's head knocker.

A few seconds passed and then Cameron was there, opening up, and a little girl with long red locks was appearing behind him. This had to be Rosie—she was the spitting image of her father.

'Hi.'

'Hey. Come on in.'

He stepped back and Rosie grabbed Grace's hand to rush her off to her bedroom to play.

Bethan had hoped that the girls would stay with them for a while, to keep the conversation and the atmosphere pleasant, but with the girls gone she rubbed at her arms and looked about the place, surprised to see such a homely home.

'This is beautiful.'

'Thanks. Can I get you a drink? Tea? Coffee? Something a wee bit stronger?'

Something a bit stronger would be perfect. To settle her nerves. A wee dram of whisky knocked back in one gulp, perhaps?

'Er...tea, please.'

'Milk and one sugar, right?'

'Yes, thank you.'

She followed him through to the kitchen. Every room she entered made her wish she had a home like this one. There was an inglenook fireplace with an old Aga, and copper pots and pans hanging from a rack on the ceiling along with sprays of dried flowers. There was even a tray of freshly baked cookies on the side, cooling under a white-netted cloche.

He bakes?

She wanted to tell him that she thought the place was amazing. That *he* was amazing. But the words stayed clogged up in her throat, refusing to come out.

'Take a seat. I won't be long.'

She sat and watched him bustle about the kitchen. He knew his way around it perfectly, and served them a tray of tea with a side plate of the freshly baked biscuits.

'Apple and cinnamon.' He offered her one.

'Thanks.' She took one and tucked it in beside her cup. 'I never imagined you as the kind of man who dons an apron.' She smiled at him.

Cam laughed and pointed at what looked like a yellow apron hanging on the back of a door. 'If it makes you feel any better, I didn't actually put it on.'

'Shame. I bet yellow is your colour.'

'With *this* hair? No.' He smiled.

She took a bite of the biscuit. It was soft and crumbly, with chunks of soft apple and a hint of spice to warm the palate afterwards. 'They're good.'

'I've had time to practise.'

'You'll have even more when you leave work.'

He nodded, looking uncomfortable.

She put the cookie down. 'This seems very odd.'

'Yeah.' He smiled ruefully.

Neither of them spoke for a moment, and the tension between them hung in the air like a thick fog. Neither of them was sure how to make a start in the conversation.

When it became clear that Cam couldn't start it off, she decided to take a step.

'So…your grandfather said some pretty startling things today.'

A nod. 'He did.'

'He accused me of stepping into a dead man's shoes. Said that you were…dying.'

She said it quietly, pausing for a moment to study his face—the weariness that was now in his eyes, the dark shadows beneath. He looked like a pale Scottish vampire.

'What did he mean? I need to know if I'm to help you.'

Death was not a new thing to Bethan. She was accustomed to hearing about it. About hearing diagnoses, delivering them herself. She just hadn't expected to hear it from him.

'I don't want to be a burden to anyone. I know you've had enough of that in your life already. I wasn't going to tell you anything.'

'You were going to try and keep this secret?'

He nodded again. 'It seemed the best way.' He

sounded resigned to his fate. 'When you told me about your husband, I knew I couldn't let you know about me.'

'So it's true?'

'Yes.'

'What is it?' She felt a churning deep in her stomach.

He sighed and gazed back at her, considering his answer. 'It's a high grade-four glioma, near my optic nerve. They say it's near impossible to operate on. That I have probably less than a year left. A year I want to spend with Rosie.'

A glioma. Brain cancer. *Dammit.*

Her face flushed hot. Her mind flooded with knowledge about the condition, all that she knew rushing to the forefront as if a dam had burst. This wasn't fair! A surge of anger almost overwhelmed her, but as her mind raced she remained calm outwardly, like a swan on the surface of the water.

'What symptoms do you have?'

'I get headaches and nausea. Mood swings. They tell me I might lose my sight, if it invades the optic nerve—which it probably will do, seeing as it's fast-growing and aggressive.'

Cancer. Damn!

'Cameron...' She reached out to lay her hand on his. An instinctive gesture. She needed to make contact, to give comfort. She wasn't worrying about it being misunderstood—she just needed to touch him. To make him know that he wasn't alone. And it felt good. It felt *right*.

She met his gaze and saw that he was staring at her hand on his. As if he wasn't used to it. As if she'd done the oddest thing possible. Had she made him uncomfortable? She withdrew it.

Cameron cleared his throat and got to his feet and began to pace the kitchen. 'Before you ask, I've had chemo and radiotherapy. There's nothing more to be done.'

'I can't believe this. It seems so unfair.'

'Life isn't fair—as *you* know all too well.'

'They can't operate? Not at all? Surely they could remove *some* of it?'

'It would just keep growing back. And the trauma on my body of countless operations—'

'But if it gave you more time—'

'What would be the quality of that extra time if it was spent in a hospital bed? What's the point of all that if it just gives me more time hooked up to a drip, feeling like I'm at death's door anyway? I don't want Rosie seeing me like that.'

'No…of course not.'

But her mind was racing, thinking of who she knew—who might be able to help. Friends of friends…colleagues of colleagues. Someone must know *something* to give this man more time with his child. To give Rosie more time to make memories with her father. To give *her* more time with him.

She liked him. Liked this man. Her colleague. Her employer. She sensed that he would be a good friend if they had the time to develop their friendship. He was a decent man. Kind and caring. She didn't want to lose him. She'd just met him.

I'm staring at him.

She looked away. Away from those blue eyes of his. Eyes that held such intelligence and yet also sorrow and resignation and regret. They were haunting. One look saw far too much.

'Don't be sad for me, Bethan. I don't need pity.'

'How can I not be sad when this doesn't seem fair?'

From the other room, they heard the delightful sounds of laughter from the two girls. Two girls enjoying life and having fun.

'Many things aren't fair. But we make the best of them because of those we love. Right now my daughter is in the other room and she doesn't know—fully—what's coming. I tried to tell her. To prepare her. But I couldn't say the words. I just said I was ill and I would have to go away. For ever. Do you know what she said? She said, *"Daddy, you're a doctor. You can make yourself better."* When I told her that I couldn't, that it didn't work that way and that I wasn't the indestructible superhero she'd always imagined me to be, she got angry. And I had to let her be angry, so she could process it.'

He sighed again. 'Now *you* need to process it. I know it stinks—*I know this*—and so do you.

But we need to make the best of it. For our own peace of mind.'

She knew he was right. But that didn't make it any better. More than anything she wanted to get on her computer and start researching this. There had to be something they could do. A medical trial? Some new research?

But, more than anyone, she knew the poisonous touch of hope. Hope made you think you could escape something bad. Hope made you an optimist. Made you think anything was possible. And when you finally realised that there was no point in hope... That was the crash. The deep, agonising roar of pain and depression as hope receded and reality punched its way into your life.

People thought they could cheat death. They always tried. Especially doctors.

'Let me help you, Cam.'

'I don't need you to be my doctor. Just my friend.'

She leaned forward, emphatic. '*I am* your friend.'

He sat down again and he reached for *her* hand

this time. Squeezed her fingers in a thank-you gesture. *Thanks for saying that. I appreciate it.*
That was all it was.
Right?
So why was her heart beating so fast?

CHAPTER FIVE

THEY WERE A week into working together. Bethan found herself concentrating hard on work, but also concentrating hard on keeping an eye on Cam. Each morning he arrived to work with her she would ask him the same question.

'How are you feeling today?'

To begin with he'd borne her concern well, but by the third day he'd begun to lose patience.

'You don't have to check on me every day, you know!'

'I'm sorry. I'm just concerned about you, that's all. How could I not be?'

He'd looked a little abashed then. Rubbed his face with his hands. 'I'm sorry, too. I shouldn't have bitten your head off like that. Can we start again?'

And she had smiled, nodded. Keen for them to be on good terms.

In between patients she would turn to him and engage him in conversation, trying to keep their conversation bright and chirpy.

She'd found during the time she'd spent with Ashley that keeping a positive mental attitude had helped a lot—for both of them—so she was applying it to this situation. It was better than dwelling on the alternative. Plus, she was feeling on edge. Finding herself in such a situation again. She wanted to help. To do something. But Cam seemed resigned to his fate, so she wasn't sure what was best to do. His moods swung wildly from day to day. Sometimes he was short of temper, and at other times he was the sweetest guy ever!

As he had been with what had happened with Andy Glen.

Andy had come in with a severe cough that he'd had for at least two weeks.

Bethan had listened to his chest, taken his temperature, but everything had seemed normal enough. There had been no extraneous sounds in his lungs...his chest had seemed clear.

'It's just a virus, Mr Glen. I know it's miserable, but you're just going to have to wait for it to clear on its own.'

Mr Glen had not looked happy with that response. 'You what? I've been coughing my guts up for a bloody fortnight—you think I'm going to keep on doing that? Give me some antibiotics!' His voice had risen with irritation and anger.

'Antibiotics won't make the slightest bit of difference to you, Mr Glen. In fact, they could even make you worse.'

'Don't give me that old rubbish! I've been watching the news. I've seen you doctors, trying to cut back on how many you give out. It's all about the money, ain't it? Rather than people!'

'I can assure you, Mr Glen—'

Mr Glen had stood up, his face a mask of anger, ready to rain down a storm of abuse and bile.

Bethan had shrunk back in her chair, but before she'd been able to do anything Cameron had leapt to his feet and taken Mr Glen by the arm.

'You need to calm down, Andy!' he'd said. His voice firm and brooking no nonsense.

'Calm down? Why should I?'

'Because I won't tolerate abuse in this surgery,

and your treatment of a doctor who is doing her best to care for you in the correct manner is rude and threatening.'

Andy had blustered for a moment, his cheeks reddening, before he had to cough again, covering his mouth with his sleeve. 'Do you hear that? All that phlegm? I can't get rid of it!'

'As Dr Monroe stated, very clearly, it will go away of its own accord.'

Andy had looked at Bethan, then back at Cameron. 'I want *you* to check me over.'

'There's no need. Dr Monroe has done a thorough examination.'

Andy had shrugged off Cameron's hand, still on his arm. Then, glaring at the pair of them, he'd stormed out, slamming the door behind him for good measure.

Cameron had turned to her immediately. 'Are you all right?'

She'd nodded, a little shaken.

It was hard sometimes. Patients came to see their doctors determined to come away with pills, or creams, or *something* to make them feel something was being done. But in lots of cases nothing *could* be done, and in the case of most viruses they had to burn out by themselves.

She'd forgotten what it was like to face an angry patient.

'Thank you for that.'

He'd sat back in his chair behind her. 'It's a problem sometimes. I guess the one thing I haven't shown you is the red button.'

She'd raised her eyebrows.

'Look under your desk.'

She'd done so, and spotted a discreet red button situated to the far right.

'It's a silent panic button. I had it installed a while back, for cases such as this. When I was going through chemo, and often felt weak or ill, some patients tried to take advantage and I didn't have the strength to see off the ones who got a little *demonstrative*. Press it and it will bring people running in. In case you need it when I'm no longer here.'

It was thoughtful. And just the kind of thing she'd expect a kind and considerate man like him to do. She hated the fact that people had tried to take advantage of his sickness to better their own interests.

She'd smiled at him. 'Thanks.'

She didn't want to think of him as *no longer here.* That just seemed so terribly final.

She'd put out a few feelers. Contacted other doctors she knew, asked them for their opinions. But they'd come back to her to say that they couldn't really give a definitive answer without seeing Cameron's scans and reports—which she knew were on the system, but she also knew she couldn't share them with anyone without his approval. She'd looked at them herself, of course, and had felt her heart sinking on seeing them.

But she was only a GP. Not a neurosurgeon. What did she know about it for sure?

At the end of morning surgery, before they went into lunch, she turned to him and smiled.

Cameron raised a suspicious eyebrow at her. 'Okay, what's going on?'

'Cam, I've been thinking a lot just lately. About your situation and I've got in touch with a few people...' She saw him roll his eyes and then he sat back in his chair, his arms folded, as he listened out of politeness. 'They're people who might be able to help, but they'd need to see your scans and medical history and I wondered if—'

'No, Bethan.'

'But, if it could help…'

'No one can help me! Do you think I've not tried to find a way out of this situation? Do you think I'm just rolling over and waiting to die? That some quack told me I have a year and I've just gone, *Oh, okay, fine!* I've *looked*. I've *searched*. I've found nothing.'

'But how long ago was that? A month? Two months? You know things can change quickly in medicine—advances are being made all the time! I know a colleague in Edinburgh who's doing amazing deep brain laser surgery. Please let me show him your scans.'

'I don't see the point.'

'Well, I do!'

A small smidgen of anger entered her tone and she blushed at hearing it. Shouting at her boss? She took a breath. And another. Allowing herself a moment to get that back under control.

'If they say they can't help, then you haven't

lost anything, have you? But if they say there might be something, then...' She let Cameron fill in the blanks in his own head. The implication was there. A chance. Maybe. Who knew, if they didn't try? She knew she was walking him down that road of hope again, but it might be worth it.

Cameron sighed and got up out of his chair to pace the small room.

She watched him and waited, hoping desperately that he would say yes. He was such a wonderful man. She really liked him and he had a wicked sense of humour. Some of the jokes he had told her over the past few days!

And he'd kept her buoyed up when she'd had to treat old Jenna Jackson and her advanced Motor Neurone Disease; he'd passed her tissues when she'd cried after spending an hour with a woman who'd recently miscarried.

'It's going to be okay,' he'd said. 'Are you all right?'

She'd sniffed, dabbing at her nose. 'It's just so *sad*. She really wanted that baby. To see her break down like that...'

Just remembering the woman weeping in front

of her had set Bethan off again. It had reminded her of the time she'd thought she was miscarrying Grace, having an early bleed. She'd never felt so much fear. Never felt so much terror. She'd been lucky. She hadn't lost her baby. But her poor patient had.

She'd leaned into Cameron in that brief moment, appreciating his strength and warmth, his arm around her shoulder as he'd waited for her to gather herself, the truly strange feeling of having someone support *her* for a change.

So why wouldn't he let her do the same for him?

'Fine. Go ahead,' he said now.

'Really?' A smile broke out across her features and she jumped from her chair like an excited schoolgirl and pulled him to her for a hug.

It was just meant to be a thank-you. She stood there, wrapped in his arms as he laughed with her, and then the laughter stopped and she realised. *I don't want to let him go.* She was pressed up against his body and how good that felt.

Guilt rushed through her with the strength and power of a tsunami and she quickly let him go.

Blushing. Hot. Unable to meet his gaze, which she could feel upon her.

I've overstepped the mark.

She glanced up at him. Once. Her Princess Diana look, Nanna had once called it. Tucked her hair behind her ear. 'Thanks.'

He swallowed, staring at her, seemingly just as shocked as she was. 'It's okay.'

Bethan sank back down into her chair and for the want of nothing else to do powered down the computer so they could go to lunch.

Being up against Cameron had felt so good! The feel of a strong, powerful man in her arms again had been... She couldn't think of the words. All she knew was that it had felt good. He had *smelt* good. She had felt his hands upon her—one on her shoulder blade, the other in the small of her back—and it had suddenly felt as if his hands were made of blazing fire and her skin was being seared by his touch, even through her clothes.

Awareness of this man... Cameron Brodie...

Am I falling for him? Forget all that. That's not why you're here. Concentrate on the fact that you've got his permission.

'Right... I...er... I guess we ought to go for lunch.'

'Aye, we ought to.'

He seemed just as unsure as she did. Awkward. Uncomfortable. She'd practically thrown herself at him—he must have wondered what the hell was going on.

It was embarrassing. She didn't know what had got into her. But she felt a fire inside her. A fire that needed feeding in her pursuit to help Cam fight his condition. Because she wasn't ready to let him go. She felt there was a chance with him. A chance she and Ashley had never had. There was time.

I really like him.

They'd just met. She was only just getting to know him. And it wasn't fair that someone so lovely could possibly be taken from her.

Again.

Was that it? Was her psyche, her heart, fed up with being robbed? Life had taken her parents from her. It had taken Ashley. And she had returned to Gilloch to start anew. A fresh beginning, away from all that trauma and pain. And now life was trying it on again. By threatening to take Cam. By threatening to make her play out the same role in the same horrifying nightmare.

She wanted to fight it. She wanted to win! Surely it was her turn? Because death wasn't supposed to be here in Gilloch for her. This place was about life and love. The open, loving arms of her grandmother. Her birthplace. New friends.

Cameron Brodie.

She had to admit, even if only to herself, that she felt something for him. She knew it was true—there was no point in denying it. Maybe if it had been different circumstances, then…

But the way he looked at her. Those sparkling blue eyes. The way he laughed—so open and warm. Genuine. He was a gentleman. Kind. A good listener. A great doctor.

And she wanted more time with him.

A year would not be enough.

She had to fight for him.

It was what a friend would do.

He knew she was just trying to help. Just doing her job in the best interests of a patient. Only he *wasn't* her patient. He was her colleague. Her boss. Her...*what?*

It felt like something more.

She had been right. Absolutely right when she'd told him at her interview that she got attached quickly. Emotionally involved. He could see that in her eyes. A fiery determination to beat his diagnosis, as if she was some crazy magician who had one last rabbit to draw out of the hat.

But he was disturbed. More disturbed than he had been in a long time. And he was a man who had heard he only had a year to live recently.

Something was happening between them. He could feel it. A small flame of something, burning quietly in the background. They were both studiously trying to ignore it—because he was *dying*, and what was the point in getting involved with someone? Especially someone who'd lost her own husband to cancer?

He couldn't put her through all that again, though he felt instinctively that she was prepared to do it. He knew what it was like to stand by a graveside and weep. He knew what it was like to miss someone so much you often felt as if you couldn't breathe.

He had to keep a distance between them. So sudden hugs when they were alone together were not a good idea! The way she'd felt in his arms had been... He shook his head to try and clear the image. She'd felt so good! He'd leaned his head on top of hers and inhaled the scent of her hair, and his eyes had closed in delight as he'd squeezed her tighter against him.

It had been a subconscious response, he hadn't realised he was doing it, and she had jumped out of his arms so fast!

He missed holding a woman. He missed having someone to lean on. To share things with. And, although she'd only been with him for a week, he'd found himself telling her things he hadn't expected.

Bethan was so easy to talk to—she invited confidences. Just last week he'd told her about some of the things he had on his Bucket List. He'd looked at her sheepishly.

'It's not daredevil stuff. It's nothing amazingly brilliant, like some people want. It's more the simple things, small pleasures—watching the sunrise; learning how to play the piano; falling in love one last time...'

He'd blushed at that last one. He hadn't meant to share it. It was an intensely private wish that he'd thought he would never admit out loud. But he missed what he'd had with his wife, and this diagnosis made him feel so alone—even though he had Rosie and his family. He was lonely. Separate from everyone else. He yearned for those heady days of falling in love, but knew it would never happen again—because who would fall for a man with a death sentence?

And who said you had to fall in love with a person? You could fall in love with a language, with food, with music. It could be anything! He just hadn't explained it properly.

Blushing, he'd found himself tongue-tied when he'd seen the look on her face.

She'd smiled at him. 'I think those things sound wonderful. And you never know...'

'Well, I know about that last one.'

'Why not? Why couldn't you fall in love again?'

'It would be unfair to the other person. I couldn't allow it. No matter how much I wanted it.'

He'd liked sitting with Bethan, chatting easily to her, seeing her beautiful smile and hearing her gentle laughter, aware of her caring nature, her ability to invite people to talk and confess their inner secrets...

But he felt bare in front of her now. A wee bit exposed. He wasn't ungrateful for her help, the fact that she was still trying, but he'd done that part—denial. He had raged against his diagnosis, had been determined that *somehow* he would find someone to help him.

He hadn't.

And that had been the difficult part. Having every specialist he'd asked tell him that they were very sorry, but there was nothing they could do. That he had to accept it and live his life the best way he could. Let go of hope.

So, he might not allow himself to fall in love, but it did look as if he would bow out of this life with one amazing brand-new friend at his side... and the idea of that pleased him.

He'd been so determined to keep everyone out. To put up fences, barriers. To keep his distance, make his passing less painful for those who worked with him or knew him.

It would be different for his family, of course. For his father, burying his only son. For Rosie, losing her father. He could not make it better for them, but he could damn well make it better for everyone else.

And now he had Bethan. She was different, somehow. She understood. She *knew* what he was going through without him having to say.

He hadn't realised how much he'd needed that. How much he needed *her*.

He wanted to embrace it so badly!

But he was terrified of what it might ultimately mean…

Cameron kissed his grandmother on the cheek. 'How is the old monster?'

'Itchy. And grumpy. As per usual.'

He smiled. 'Thought I'd come and check on

him. See how he's doing with the antibiotics Bethan prescribed.'

'He's doing well. And the rash hasn't got any worse.'

His grandmother began to brew a new pot of tea.

'I thought she was very nice, Dr Monroe. 'tis a shame your grandfather bit her head off the way he did. If he hadn't been so ill I would have given him a clout. Shameful behaviour, it was.'

'You won't hear me disagreeing with you.'

He settled onto a kitchen chair, feeling weary after a long day at the surgery. Bethan was doing very well now. She knew her way through the practice computer like a hacker. He even suspected she knew how to make it do a few things that even *he* didn't know about! And everyone was warming to her charm, her ready smile and listening ear. He'd made a very good choice.

'And how are *you* doing, laddie?'

'Not bad, considering.'

'Where's Rosie?'

'She's at Bethan's. Play date.'

She smiled. 'Let's not mention that wee bit of info to your granda'.'

He laughed. 'No.'

His grandmother studied him as she set down the tea before him. 'She's a bonny lass.'

'Rosie?'

'Dr Monroe.'

'Is she? I hadn't noticed,' he lied, sipping from his hot drink and hoping that his grandmother would change the subject and not notice the flare of heat he felt in his cheeks. Hopefully she would put it down to the steaming tea.

'Mhairi must be very pleased to have her back in the fold.'

'I know.'

And then, as was the way with some people of the older generation, even though they'd already told you a story once, they wanted to tell it again.

'They used to go out together. Your granda' and Mhairi. They were quite the lovebirds, by all accounts.'

'I remember him saying.'

His grandmother looked rueful. 'They always say you never forget your first love, don't they?'

Did she think her husband still had a thing for Bethan's nanna? Had she been upset that his grandfather had asked after Mhairi after all these years?

He peered at her closely. 'He's *your* first love, though, isn't he?'

She smiled and nodded, her cheeks flushed. 'Aye. He is.'

Cameron felt the need to reassure her. 'He does love you, you know. Just because you weren't his first love, it doesn't mean he loves you any less.'

'I know.' She patted his hand and looked at him. 'And just because you've had one great love, it doesn't mean you can't have another.'

Cam frowned. 'What do you mean?'

She laughed. 'You'll work it out, laddie.'

He looked down at the old kitchen table, in-grained and scored by decades of wear and tear. Was she saying he could still have a chance to fall in love? Despite the ticking of the clock? Who would be foolish enough to give him that?

'So…do you want to go upstairs and say hello to the old stick-in-the-mud?'

He looked up, laughed and nodded. 'Why not?'

Bethan was drinking pretend tea out of a small pink plastic tea cup with Grace and Rosie in her daughter's bedroom.

The two girls had been merrily playing outside in Nanna's back garden for a while, but the already overcast skies had started to darken and grumble and so they'd come indoors, looking for something to do. Now they all sat around a small table, sipping their 'tea' with dolls and teddies in attendance.

'Mummy, do we have any cake?' asked Grace.

'I'm not sure. Shall I go and check?'

'Yes, please.'

She hurried downstairs, glad for the chance to stretch her legs and her back, aching from being seated on the floor. There wasn't any cake downstairs, but she did find a half-packet of biscuits, so decided to take those upstairs.

As she got closer to her daughter's room she

could hear the two girls chatting, and she slowed
to listen when she heard Rosie's voice.

'I don't have a mummy like you do.'

'You don't have a mummy?'

'No. Just a daddy.'

She heard Grace sigh. 'I don't have a daddy.'

'My daddy is going to go away soon.'

'On holiday?'

'No. Just away. And he won't be coming back.'

'Who will be your daddy, then?'

'Grandpa Doug. I'm going to live with him. I
like it there, he has dogs.'

'I wish we had a dog. I love animals.'

'Me, too.'

Bethan could feel her heart pounding in her
chest. She hadn't known how much Rosie knew,
but clearly Cameron had tried to talk with her
about the future. It was heartbreaking, listening
to the two girls chat about something so huge and
life-changing, and she had to fight her instinct to
rush inside Grace's bedroom and pull both girls
into her arms and hug them.

'I know,' Grace said. 'You could come and live
with us!'

Bethan chose that moment to head back in, before *that* conversation could develop.

'I've got biscuits!' she declared, waving the packet before her, hoping that the promise of a sugary snack would steer the conversation back onto safer ground.

'Mummy? Could Grace come and live with us when her daddy goes away?'

'Oh, I'm not sure, honey...'

'Or you could marry Rosie's daddy and then we'd both have a mummy and a daddy.'

Oh, dear. The biscuit thing clearly hadn't worked.

She felt her cheeks flush and her jaw work as she fumbled for the right thing to say. She sighed with relief when, downstairs, the doorbell rang. *Saved by the bell.*

'Let me see who that is,' she said.

Nanna was out. She'd popped round to see Vera Cromarty to pick up a book, and had no doubt stopped for a tea and natter. Gratefully, she ran down the stairs to see who it was.

She pulled open the door. 'Cameron! Hi, come on in.'

'Thanks. How's it gone?'

Bethan hadn't realised how quickly the time had passed. A quick glance at the clock in the hallway showed that it was seven p.m.—the time he'd said he'd pick up Rosie.

'Good! The girls have loved it. They really are very good friends. Rosie's been no bother at all. I hardly noticed she was here.'

Which was a lie, because of course she'd noticed. Wanting to make sure the little girl had a good time, she'd hovered in the background to keep an eye on both of them. She hadn't been able to help it, knowing she was responsible for Cameron's little girl.

She had watched Rosie play, marvelling at that gloriously long red hair of hers, at her bright blue eyes so like her father's. She'd studied her, looking for signs of her mother, wondering which of her traits had been passed down.

'That's great. Thanks for having her over.'

'Are you kidding? Grace wouldn't stop asking me. I hope you've had a pleasant couple of hours in peace?'

'Kind of. I went to see my grandparents.'

She nodded. 'Oh. How is Angus? Coping okay?'

'He is. As well as can be expected.'

Bethan ushered him through to the kitchen rather than have him standing in the hallway. She proffered a chair and sat opposite.

'Does he need me to pop in again?' She would do it if she had to, no matter what. If her patient needed her…

'No, he's doing okay.'

'That's good. I might give him a ring at some point, then. Just to check in.'

'He'd probably like that.'

Cam smiled and she knew he meant the opposite. Some people just didn't like doctors, but Angus Brodie was a different fish-filled kettle!

Behind them, they both heard a key in the front door. Nanna was back.

Bethan smiled. 'I'll get the kettle on.'

'That'll be lovely, lassie. Vera can't half chat, and she makes a lousy brew.' Nanna bustled into the kitchen and smiled at Cameron. 'Och, hello, pet.'

'Hello, Mhairi.' He stood and smiled at her.

Nanna looked at both of them, a smile on her

face. 'So what have you two lovebirds been chatting about, then?'

'Nanna!'

Mhairi chuckled to herself. 'Och, don't mind me, I'm just playing with you.'

Cameron smiled at them both, the ultimate gentleman, politeness personified. 'I'd better get going. See if I can tear my wee lass away.'

Bethan stood up, too. 'They're in Grace's room.' She followed him to the bottom of the stairs. 'Girls? Rosie? Your dad's here to take you home.'

'I want to stay here!' Rosie called down.

'Come on, Rosie. We must be off, if you're to have a bath before bed.'

There were some gentle grumbling noises from Grace's bedroom and then the two girls came trotting down the stairs, both smiling.

Rosie threw herself into her daddy's arms. Bethan smiled at the two of them. Their easy nature with each other. It was clear to anyone that they had a great relationship. One that would soon be soured when Cam's health deteriorated.

'Thanks once again for having her over.'

'It was no trouble.'

'Perhaps I could cook you dinner as a thank-you, one night? Maybe this Friday? After my last day at work? You can celebrate getting rid of me.'

Dinner. With Cameron. At his place.

Her heart thudded. She knew Nanna would be listening and putting two and two together and coming up with four hundred.

'Oh...er...'

'It's just a thank-you. For everything, really. Come on—say yes. I promise I can cook as well as bake. I'm not going to give you a ready meal from the microwave.'

She didn't know what to say to this sudden surge of friendliness. She wanted to say yes, but she knew if she spent an hour or two staring at this man across a table her feelings for him would intensify. But if she said no that would be rude and would make their time together awkward.

'All right. That would be lovely, thank you.'

'Okay. Say seven o clock?'

'Perfect.' She waved them both goodbye from the front doorstep, watching as Cam opened the car door for his daughter and made sure she was strapped in properly before getting into the driver's seat. He was such a good father. And a great doctor. An amazing man. He was so brave in what he was facing.

She'd spent hours each night, sitting up in bed with her laptop on her lap, scrolling through websites and published medical papers on gliomas, surgeries and morbidity rates. She would always fall asleep exhausted, her mind running through tables of figures and trial data.

Easy bedtime reading it was not. But she was determined to find something that would help him. Even if it was just some extra time with his daughter. Rosie deserved it. *He* deserved it.

Cam gave her one last wave and a cheery smile as he drove away, and Bethan became aware of her nanna standing close behind. 'I suppose you heard that.'

'Heard what, lass?' Nanna asked.

'Hmm…' Bethan closed the front door and raised an eyebrow as she turned to face her. 'Really?'

Nanna's face was the perfect mask of innocence. Except for her all-knowing smile.

* * *

She couldn't quite believe it. Her two weeks with Cam were nearly up. This was to be their last day working together. One last day of appointments in the surgery.

Two weeks ago she'd yearned to be at the stage when she would work unaccompanied. Had ached for the moment when she would take over fully, flying solo as the only doctor in Gilloch.

Now she had other thoughts. Other feelings. Perhaps some she didn't want to examine too closely.

She felt a responsibility for Cam's wellbeing. Was watching over him. Perhaps it was because that had been her role with Ashley—who knew?—but she felt the need to keep an eye on him. And with him not being around after today she was beginning to feel a little anxiety creeping in.

Time had gone so quickly. She'd enjoyed sharing his workspace, his patients, working together with him, talking with each other, discussing patients, breaking down their method of approach to each case.

Alone, they had made each other smile and laugh, and she had been bowled over by his kindness, his commitment to his work. And that was made even more evident now, when he arrived in the surgery with a sheaf of papers—detailed lists of what he had to do each day, each week, each month and each year, so that she wouldn't miss anything.

'In case there's something I've forgotten, Janet should be able to point you in the right direction—or the office manager, of course.'

'Thank you for these, Cam, they're great.'

He looked pale again today. More so than he had before. She didn't want to start her day with the same question she asked him every day, but his pallor, forced it from her lips.

'How are you doing today?'

He shrugged. 'So-so.'

'If you're not well you could go home and get some rest, whilst Rosie is at school, and we could do dinner another day.'

She was trying to make it easier for him. Trying to lighten the load. She remembered what it had been like for Ashley when he'd forced himself into doing activities when he'd felt poorly, simply exhausting himself and making himself worse.

'It's all right. I promised you two weeks and two weeks I will do. Besides, I'm just going to be sitting in that chair. It's not as if I'm operating on someone. I've taken my painkillers—they'll kick in soon.'

'Well, if you're sure?'

'I'm sure.'

'Let me at least check your blood pressure.' She bent to pick up the cuff.

'No!' he snapped, instantly looking aghast at the way he'd raised his voice to her. 'Sorry. I'm fine. You don't need to check on me.'

Was it simply anger? Irritation? Or was it a sign of the mood swings that gliomas could cause? She'd read about those—that as the glioma grew it could cause uncharacteristic behaviour and mood swings. It could cause patients to be reckless—and fearless, too.

He'd never raised his voice to her before. He had always been gently spoken. Wonderfully so, with that soft Scottish burr.

He looked appalled with himself. 'I'm sorry, I...'

'It's okay.'

'No, it's not. I...' He let out a sigh. 'It was appalling behaviour. I guess there's a bit of Angus in me after all?' He tried a smile to lighten the joke, but it fell flat.

She was worried about him. Incredibly so.

He sank into his chair by the window and the light from the weak sunshine increased the shadows upon his face. He looked a haunted man.

She had to fight the urge to go to him and drape her arms around him, pull him close. Just to give him a hug, to show him that it was all right, that she was here, that she would help him through this. That he didn't have to fight this alone.

But she didn't.

Instead she awkwardly sank into her seat and pressed the buzzer for their first patient of their last day.

She gave him one last look, but he didn't see. He was rubbing at his face, as if weary and tired, and she had to look away again as their patient arrived.

In walked Mrs McConnell, her step determined, her face meaning business.

'I'm not here about me, Doctor, I'm here about my husband, Don.'

'Oh? What appears to be the trouble?'

'He's driving me mad, I tell you. Every time I speak to him I have to repeat myself three times, four times, because the daft old beggar can't hear me! He's gone deaf. But will he come to see you to have it checked out? Will he heck!'

Bethan smiled. She could imagine it would drive someone batty if they had to keep repeating themselves.

'Well, he really needs to make an appointment, Mrs McConnell. I can't check him out like this. Would he let me visit him at home? He might just need his ears syringed.'

Mrs McConnell sighed. 'Would you do that? Visit him at home? I wouldn't tell him in advance, though—he'd go out and leave me in the lurch. We'll keep it a surprise from him.'

Bethan understood, but she wasn't fond of surprising someone at home. 'It might be best if he *does* know, Mrs McConnell. I'd hate him to think we were ganging up on him.'

'Ganging up on him is much better than me whacking him over the head with a frying pan, lassie! Which I'm sorely tempted to do right now!'

Bethan made an appointment on the system and put Don McConnell on her home visit list.

Her first home visits without Cam.

Mrs McConnell took a closer glance at Cam. 'Perhaps you ought to put this one on your list, too. He looks a wee bit peaky again.'

'Oh, don't you worry, Mrs McConnell. I'll be keeping a good firm eye on him.'

Her patient nodded glumly. 'What would these men do without us, huh?'

CHAPTER SIX

THE QUESTION WAS, what to wear for dinner at Cam's house?

It was a thank-you dinner, a goodbye dinner, a handing-over-the-reins dinner, and she wanted to look as if she'd made an effort—but she didn't want to look as if she was dressing up for a man. Nanna would spot it a mile off, for a start, and—as she kept telling herself—she was not trying to date Cam. She was not trying to attract him in any way.

So why was she standing in front of her wardrobe, yet again, wondering what to wear? She had plenty of smart casual clothes that she wore for work and every day, but hardly any *going out* clothes.

There had never been any reason to go out for years—she'd just looked after Grace and stayed at home. Occasionally she'd go to a friend's house, but that had always been a girlfriend's house and that was different.

There was one dress in her wardrobe that was smart enough for dinner, but she didn't know whether she should wear it…

'Just wear the damn dress, Bethan,' she muttered to herself, grabbing at the hanger and slipping into it, pulling up the side zipper and twisting and turning in front of the mirror to make sure it still looked okay.

She'd lost some weight. Stress, probably.

By the time she made it downstairs she was wearing make-up and heels and dangly earrings, and she stood awkwardly in front of Mhairi, waiting for some acerbic comment.

'You look very nice, lass.'

'That's it? *Nice?*'

Nanna nodded. 'Aye.'

'You don't think it's too…flirty?'

'Well, what do *you* think?'

Bethan lifted her chin, determined to stand her ground. 'I think it strikes the right balance of professional, smart and feminine. It's a dress that I'm wearing because it suits me and nobody else.'

She gave one firm nod of her head. 'And it's not *for* anyone else.'

'Okay, then.'

'Right, well… I'll be off. You'll call me if I'm needed? If Grace doesn't settle?' Bethan picked up her mobile and slipped it into her bag.

'She'll be fine. *We'll* be fine. Now, get off with you. Time's a-ticking.'

It was. And she still hadn't told Nanna that Cameron was sick.

'I'll see you later, then.'

The lamb shanks were roasting nicely in the oven, filling the cottage with a delicious aroma. The steamer was quietly cooking the baby potatoes and assorted veggies, and in the fridge sat a tiramisu that had been made with a few wee drams of the Scotch his granda' had given him.

He'd almost given in and got a shop-bought dessert. He felt so exhausted today. So tired. The pain in his head had been quietly hammering away all day, with the painkillers not really doing much to touch it. He hoped he would improve tomorrow. He hoped that this was not going to be the state of affairs for the rest of his time left on this earth.

He'd snapped at not just Bethan today, but also Janet, when she'd asked him to sign off on some prescriptions as he was on his way out of the door. And then at Rosie, when she'd nagged him over and over about getting a puppy, because a friend at school had just got one and it was, *'The only thing she wanted in the whole, wide world, ever. Pleeeease?'*

She'd just not let it go! And he'd turned on her like an ogre, roaring at her to go to her room.

Afterwards he'd felt so guilty. He'd knocked on her bedroom door and asked if he was allowed in, and when she had let him come in he'd found her cross-legged on her bed, her face stained with tears.

That had almost broken his heart.

But not enough to grant her wish of having a puppy. Puppies took commitment and time, and time wasn't on his side. Having a puppy wasn't his decision to make any more. He'd need to ask his father, because he'd be the one looking after Rosie when he was gone. He'd be the one to do the dog's toilet training and feed it and pay any vet's bills. He couldn't lump that on him—it wasn't fair.

Afterwards he'd got Rosie to help him in the kitchen and they'd made the tiramisu together. It had earned him a few Brownie points with his daughter and she'd eventually gone up to her room to read alone, knowing he was having Bethan over for dinner.

'Is Grace coming, too? Could she have a sleepover?'

'No, it's just Bethan. Maybe another time?'

He'd taken some more of his painkillers and had a bit of a tidy-up, showered and put on some dark trousers and a white shirt. He couldn't remember the last time he'd dressed up for a woman and the thought gave him pause. Was he trying too hard? Was he going to too much trouble?

This was meant to be a thank-you, a goodbye, and an it's-all-in-your-hands-now kind of thing. The last woman he'd got dressed up for had been his wife, which seemed such a long time ago. Years. Much too long a time of being alone.

Why did it feel as if he was getting ready for

a date? With those same nervous butterflies in his stomach? That same adrenaline flooding his veins? The same anticipation?

He removed the tie he'd selected and hung it back up. Took off the shoes he'd meticulously polished. *I'll do it in my socks.* Men didn't flirt that way, did they? In their socks? Besides, Bethan would probably just turn up in some old work clothes, or something. They were colleagues, and that was all.

His doorbell rang, and with it his nerves jumped into overdrive. Trotting down the stairs, he gave his reflection one last check in the hall mirror and then opened the door.

And gasped.

He hoped afterwards that he hadn't looked like a landed fish, but Bethan looked absolutely amazing. Stunning was the word. In a beautiful bright dress with one side of her lush brown hair held back by a diamond slide. Her features were accentuated by dark eyeliner and mascara, there was a faint hint of blusher on her creamy cheeks, and her lips were highlighted by a dark red slash of lipstick.

I'm in trouble.

His capacity for forming words seemed to disappear, and he wasn't entirely sure he could blame that on the glioma. Eventually he managed to close his mouth and smile, before uttering, 'You look amazing. Come on in.'

'Thanks.'

She stepped past him and he inhaled her perfume as she landed a brief kiss of greeting on his cheek. Something light and fruity, almost citrus. It did strange things to his insides and he had to take a deep breath of air to stop himself from turning her to face him, just so he could take her in with his eyes all over again.

He didn't know how much longer he had left to enjoy beautiful things, and Bethan was certainly one of those! But what was he doing? It was ridiculous.

I'm dying. I have a year left, maybe less—who knows? And what? Suddenly I'm like a horny teenager?

Perhaps it was the fact that he had so little time left? Time in which he wanted to live! To enjoy the simple things in life. The natural beauty in the world. And what was more natural than love? His internal Bucket List had it as his last hope: *to fall in love one last time.* He'd thought it impossible. He might want it, because it would feel great, but was it ethical? To do that to someone knowing he would leave them in such grief? He knew what that felt like...to lose the love of your life.

And so did Bethan.

He shook his head to try and clear it of such romantic thoughts. 'Why don't you go through to the kitchen? Can I get you a drink?'

'Oh, that reminds me...' She reached into the bag at her side and pulled from it a bottle of red wine that she handed to him. 'I didn't know what we were having, but I know this is good, so...'

He thanked her and let her lead the way, following behind her, breathing in the hints of her perfume and silently telling himself to pull it together. To get a grip!

In the kitchen, he pulled out a chair for her. 'So...drink?'

'I'll have a glass of wine, please—whatever you're having. Seeing as I'm not on call this weekend.'

He already had a bottle of red open, so he poured her a nice glass of shiraz. Then he grabbed his own glass and proposed a toast. 'To good friends and friendship. However long it may last.'

She raised her glass and took a sip of wine. 'Something smells delicious. What are we having?'

'Lamb shanks.'

'Marvellous. Is there anything I can help you with?'

He made a mock pretence of looking around him. 'Er…no, I don't think so. It all seems under control. So…how does it feel to know you're on your own from next week?'

He saw her smile, the way it lit up her eyes, the slight dimple to her right cheek. 'I'm used to being on my own.'

Idiot, Cam!

'Oh, I didn't mean—'

She held up her hands. 'It's okay—really. I know you didn't mean it like that. And neither did I. What I meant was it's how we usually work, isn't it? On our own? I have enjoyed our two weeks, though. It's been great. I shall miss you sitting beside me.'

I'll miss you, too.

But he didn't say it out loud. Before he knew her he'd been dreading these last two weeks of hand-over. Imagining days during which he'd just want to be at home with Rosie now that he'd made the decision to retire. But then he'd met Bethan, and she was delightful and charming and *interesting*, and there was so much more he wanted to know about her.

But would he ever get to have that chance? He wouldn't be spending every day with her any more. He'd be at home. The only time he'd see her would be out and about, the odd hello in the village.

He'd already decided he didn't want her as his doctor. Not because he didn't like her—far from it! He liked her *too much*, and he didn't want her having to care for him in his final days the way she'd had to with her husband.

He wanted to spare her that. He wanted her to remember him as a vital young man. One still in full control. Almost healthy. He didn't want her to see him slowly deteriorate. He wanted her final memories of him to be good ones. Of their days together at work—the jokes they'd laughed at, the moments that only they had shared.

'I'll…er…just check the veg.' He turned to poke a knife into the broccoli and baby sweetcorn. They were just about done. 'They're good. Okay, I'll just make up some gravy.'

'Should I…er…lay the table?'

What?

He turned and looked around.

Of course! The table! How on earth did I forget to do that?

He flushed bright red and let out a sigh. 'I can't believe I forgot that.'

That *was* ridiculous, wasn't it? He'd been forgetting a few things just lately—the table setting; the ketchup that Rosie preferred; her *bedtime!* Last night he'd forgotten that she always had a bath before bed, and when he'd sent her up to get into her pyjamas she'd looked at him strangely and started running her *own* bath. When he'd gone upstairs to ask her what she was doing she'd had to remind him…

The glioma. Was it affecting him? He knew it could affect mood and impulse control, but memory?

Bethan politely dismissed his lapse and asked him where everything was, and before he knew it she'd laid a beautiful table for both of them, even finding matches to light the candle she'd set in the middle. He was impressed.

He pulled the lamb shanks from the oven in their crockpot and set them to one side to rest for a moment whilst he dished up the vegetables and potatoes. He set some home-made mint sauce on the table and then served the shanks. The food sat before them, issuing clouds of steam full of delicious aroma.

'Bon appetit.'

He was smiling, realising that for the first time today his headache had gone.

He waited for her to try the food first, and when he was convinced she was eating it because she was enjoying it he tucked into his own, feeling a little more relaxed.

'This is delicious. I had no idea you were such a good cook.'

'Originally I wasn't. But when I lost my wife, Holly, I had to learn. Porridge and beans on toast just wasn't going to cut it any more. Not with a growing bairn.'

She smiled and nodded. 'I know what you mean. I was never the greatest of cooks either. Ashley loved to be in the kitchen, but in those final days I had to take over and try to make him delicious things he thought he might eat. The cancer affected his appetite, and the chemo practically ruined his taste buds.' She looked up at him. 'Did it have the same effect on you? The chemo?'

'To start with. Everything tasted metallic— even water. But it's got better since I've stopped having it.'

It was a reminder that he hadn't stopped through choice but rather because his consultants had said there was no longer any point. It wasn't working, and would only make his remaining time on this earth more unpleasant.

He dabbed at his mouth and considered her from across the table. She truly was beautiful. He'd noticed it the second she'd entered his room

for her interview just a couple of weeks ago. And
he was so pleased that he had met her and em-
ployed her as his replacement. She was perfect.

But it was making him confused. He hadn't
expected this.

'Can I ask about Ashley? What he was like?'

She met his gaze and nodded. 'Sure. He was…'
She paused to think. 'He was kind and considerate—a Scorpio.' She laughed. 'He loved to play
the piano, and I used to tell him that he could've
been a professional pianist. He had such a deli-
cate touch—a real ear for music and sound. He
taught me how to play. He composed a piece
once, and every time he played it I got goose-
bumps…'

Her gaze drifted off to one side. Was she hearing that music once again?

'I wish I could have known him. Heard him
play.'

His response seemed to drag her back into the
present. 'Tell me about Holly,' she said, spearing
a floret of broccoli with her fork.

'Okay. She was a farm girl when I met her,
helping out on her parents' farm, and the first

time we met I pulled a stray piece of straw from her hair. She had hair like Rosie's, long and red, and a fiery temper to match, but we hit it off straight away. We got married, and then we found out she was expecting Rosie. We didn't think our lives could get any better.'

She was watching him, listening to him. Taking in every word. 'Can I ask…?'

'Amniotic embolism.'

Bethan closed her eyes, as if in pain, and looked down at her plate.

It was a terrible, sudden way to die. Almost without warning and too late to do anything about it. It was a rare event. Nothing that could be predicted in advance. Some of the amniotic fluid would enter the bloodstream of the mother, triggering a serious reaction that resulted in a cardio-respiratory collapse and massive bleeding.

He'd gone from being elated at the birth of his daughter to experiencing sudden pain and fear as Holly had collapsed, having not yet held her child. Cam had thought it was cruel enough to have his wife taken from him so soon. To have his daughter's mother stolen away. And then, when he'd received his own diagnosis, nothing had made much sense any more. What was the point of it all?

He'd been depressed—had even briefly entertained thoughts of just getting it over and done with himself. But he had Rosie, and knew he couldn't do that to her, so he'd soldiered on. Doing his best to fight it until he knew it was time to enjoy his last few days rather than suffer them. Hence his decision to leave work and spend time with his loved ones.

'I'm so sorry, Cameron. That must have been a terrible shock.'

'You get through it. You know that as well as I do.'

She nodded. 'I do.'

They stared into each other's eyes for a moment, two souls connecting on an intimate level. Each one bared and open to show its scars. And then the rest of the world seemed to return—the ticking of the kitchen clock, a thud from upstairs.

Cameron looked up at the ceiling. 'I'd better go

and check she's all right. Help yourself to more wine if you need it.'

Rosie was fine. She'd been building with some wooden blocks and knocked the tower down. She asked for a goodnight kiss and a hug.

'Is Bethan downstairs?'

'Yes.'

'Can I go downstairs and say hello?'

'No, but you can get into bed, like I asked you to, and go to sleep.' He kissed her on the forehead, tucked her in and closed her door behind him before going back downstairs.

Bethan was waiting for him and she'd refilled both their glasses.

'Thanks.'

'No problem.' She drew a breath. 'Are we destined to talk about death and dying, do you think? Because we've both been through so much of it?'

He smiled and nodded. 'Probably. It's common ground, if nothing else.'

'But we have something else in common.'

He frowned. 'What?'

She raised her glass in a silent toast and smiled at him. 'Surviving.'

* * *

She meant it. Surviving was more important than death. But being a survivor left you with a certain amount of guilt. A feeling of responsibility to carry on and to carry on *well*.

Like this evening, for example. Here she was with her colleague, her friend, enjoying a lovely meal. He was a great cook. And she loved being here in his home, appreciating the warmth of it, the welcome, his friendship.

He'd cooked the shanks perfectly, in a rich sauce, and the meat was just sliding off the bone and melting in her mouth. Simple things like this were to be enjoyed, because life for those left behind didn't always have to be filled with enormous things. Amazement and enjoyment could come from a sunrise, or a smile. Or a friend.

'I thought I'd call on your grandfather next week—see how he is.'

'He's doing well. I spoke to him on the phone just this morning.'

'That's good to hear.' She put down her knife and fork. 'He's very proud of you, isn't he?'

Cam smiled and nodded. 'Don't you mean *fiercely protective*?'

She laughed. 'That, too.'

'I was the first of our family to go to university. To become a doctor. My whole family had been fishermen and trawlermen. At first he didn't understand when I went away, leaving the old traditions behind, but when I came back here to Gilloch as a GP there couldn't have been anyone prouder.'

Bethan smiled at his story. 'My mother worked as a seamstress. She helped make wedding dresses. Growing up, I remember her teaching me how to sew, convinced I would work in the family shop in St Austell. But when I told her I wanted something different she supported me— as did Dad. And when I became a doctor that was how she kept introducing me to people—"This is my daughter, Bethan. *The doctor.*"' She smiled at the memory.

'I wish I could have met them.'

'They would have liked you, Cam.'

He smiled. 'It must have been hard for you to

lose them both. I can't imagine losing my father…and I guess I won't have to. He'll lose me.'

She reached for his hand and squeezed it. 'You're going to fight it, aren't you? Every step of the way?'

He swept his thumb over her knuckles, looking down at their entwined hands. 'I already have. And I'm going to fight for every extra day I can spend with Rosie.'

'What about the rest of us? Don't you want to stick around for the rest of us, too?'

Cam nodded, then glanced at her plate. 'Have you finished?'

'Yes.' Was he changing the subject?

'I'll clear the table, then.' He made to get up.

'I'll help you.'

But as she got up with him she slipped on something on the floor. Spilt water, perhaps? Something… Before she knew it she was going head over heels and grabbing onto anything that might prevent her fall.

She grabbed Cameron.

And pulled him down with her.

She hit the floor, felt a whoosh as he landed

somewhat heavily upon her—the air gone from her lungs. Her first instinct was to blush and laugh and be embarrassed at having fallen. Hoping she hadn't hurt either of them. She laughed long and hard, feeling the weight of him upon her. The weight of him against her body.

And then the laughter stopped.

The flush of embarrassment filled her cheeks, and Cam's face was so close to hers. He was staring into her eyes. His eyes were so blue, so intense, as he lay on top of her. Her hands were on his chest, but not pushing him away, just feeling its rise and fall, the accelerated beat of his heart.

'Are you okay?' she asked, her voice shaky and uncertain.

'Aye... I'm...'

And then his gaze dropped to her lips and she knew. Knew he would kiss her. Felt her own lips part as her breathing rapidly increased.

He lowered his head.

What are you doing? You shouldn't be kissing him!

A thousand different voices in her head were telling that this would end in tears. That this was not good. That this was not a good idea. The voices were loud. Screaming at her. Fuelled by doubts that came from her past.

But there was one lone voice. One pure voice in her head that was louder. And it told her she wanted this. Needed this. The feel of his lips on hers, the weight of his body upon hers.

She had not been kissed for a long time and she'd forgotten what it felt like. What it felt like to be desired. What it felt like to be seen as *a woman* and not just as a care-giver—someone who mopped a sweaty brow, controlled the medication. Someone who made the pain go away.

She sank into the kiss and a throaty murmur escaped her—she couldn't help it. The kiss was so unexpected, the feelings she was experiencing so intense and amazing. A flurry—no, a whirlwind of emotions was pulling her this way and that. Giving her what she needed in that moment.

You're kissing Cam. You shouldn't be doing that.

Oh, but it feels so good. I don't want to stop! I love how this feels. I don't want to regret something so good. We both need this.

Her fingers sank into the softness of his hair as her body thrummed at the joy of his hard, lean body against the length of hers. He'd taken his weight from her, so that she could breathe, but there was still contact between them. As if he didn't want to part from her. As if he needed this as much as she did.

The kiss intensified, became deeper, and she felt parts of her body coming alive that had been dormant for far too long. Nerve-endings were awakening, and her body was yearning for his caress, his touch, experiencing its own need to reach out and touch and explore, to find this man who had built up walls around himself for far too long.

Two lonely, hurt souls were finding solace in each other.

And then they both came up for air.

She stared into his intense blue eyes, not knowing what to say. She hoped he didn't regret it. *She* didn't. And she didn't want him to bolt. He hadn't taken advantage of her and she didn't want him to feel guilty about this.

Bethan smiled at him. 'Was that dessert?'

The corners of his mouth curved upwards. Relief?

He stood up and held out his hand for her, pulling her to her feet and then pulling her back towards him, back into his embrace, reaching up to tuck a stray strand of her hair back behind her hair.

'I don't know what that was. But I enjoyed it.'

Her cheeks flushed with heat. *Good.* So had she.

She stroked his cheek, then pulled him towards her and kissed him again.

Someone was knocking at his front door. Cam blinked hard and tried to focus on the digital clock by his bedside—five forty-eight a.m. *What the...?*

He pulled on a tee shirt and some joggers and tiptoed quietly down the stairs to unlock the door. Perhaps someone was sick? Perhaps they were calling to ask for help?

But when he opened the door he realised it wasn't anything like that.

It was Bethan, grinning like a loon, and behind her, rubbing their hands in the chill morning air, were Mhairi and Grace.

'Is everything all right?'

'Everything's perfect. The sun rises in half an hour, so get dressed—we're going out to watch it happen. Nanna will stay to look after the girls.'

He peered at Mhairi, standing behind her granddaughter, and received a smile and a nod. 'And it's brass monkeys out here, so if you could let us in we'd be most grateful!' the older woman said.

He couldn't quite believe it. She'd *remembered*? She didn't have to do this for him.

'I don't know what to say.'

Mhairi stepped forward into his house. 'You say, *Thank you very much and come on in*!'

She stalked down the hallway, Grace following her with a sleepy smile, wrapped in a blanket and clutching a teddy.

Bethan stood beside him. 'Is this okay?'

Of course it was okay. It was more than okay! Since they'd kissed a week ago his world had changed its axis. He felt brighter. More alive.

More positive than he had felt in ages! Having Bethan beside him had changed things in ways he had never suspected they could.

Oh, he had doubts. Of course he did.

What am I doing? I shouldn't be doing this to her, getting her involved with me. What can I offer her but my death?

But his need to be close to her had overridden his doubts. Just that brief taste of her that night had fired his desire to be intimate with someone again. Why *shouldn't* he live life to the full? He didn't have much time left!

I'm dying!

He was hungry to soak up every experience he could. He'd thought that keeping everyone at a distance was working, but hadn't realised just how much he actually needed.

And he needed Bethan. He was still alive for now, and life—no matter how short—needed love in it. He loved his daughter and had thought that was enough. But, no. He needed *love*, too. Not for one minute did he imagine that Bethan loved him already! But she cared for him. She had feelings for him—he could see that.

And I have feelings for her.

He'd felt her need. It matched his own. The desire to be seen as something more than what they were. These last few weeks he'd felt as if everywhere he went he had a big neon sign flashing over his head that said *Dead Man Walking!* Even though no one outside of his family and Bethan could possibly know about his death sentence. He felt it. Keenly. And his need to feel something else—something better, something *real*—was a hunger that had made him feel hollow.

With Bethan he felt full again. Fully human. A man. A man with something to give. Something to offer. Someone with value and presence.

People saw a widow and a widower and it marked out him and Bethan as characters of pity. Maybe it was all in his imagination, but...

But what people forgot was that they still had feelings. They still had thoughts and hopes for the future and their hearts still bled with pain.

We don't need pity. We need love.

That was why he'd reached out. Well, part of the reason. He was attracted to Bethan. Knew he really liked her. And quite clearly his libido still thought it was alive!

Kissing her—the feel of her, the scent of her in his arms—had almost driven him wild, and he felt sure she'd pretty much felt the same. He'd heard the sound of need, of hunger, of desire from her, and it was like a wake-up call in his head. Like a military trumpeter sounding a bugle call. A call to arms.

There'd been many more kisses since. Kisses he'd wanted to take further. He wanted to be intimate with her, but he was worried about Rosie walking in on them. Or Grace. Or Mhairi! And he also knew that if they took that extra step in their relationship there would be no going back. No putting on the brakes, no keeping her at arm's length. It would mean something more to them both.

Right now, it was still casual. He could pretend that everything was fine. Only it wasn't fine, was it? Because they were here fulfilling his Bucket List. And Bucket Lists were for people running out of time.

Bethan drove them up Mount Gillochrie to a

lay-by halfway up the mountain. She had blankets for them, and a flask of hot tea, and they opened up the large boot of her car and sat in the back, looking to the east, where the dark blue sky was beginning to fill with warmer colours.

'Thank you for this. I probably never would have done it on my own.'

'It's no problem.'

'I can't believe I'm in my thirties and I've never seen the sun rise before. Not in real life anyway. There might have been times when I was out on call and it happened, but I was always too busy to notice.'

'Life frequently makes us too busy to notice the simple things.'

He sipped at his tea. 'I guess once I've done this there are only two things left for me to do.'

She smiled. 'Learn to play the piano.'

'And fall in love again.'

Bethan flushed and looked away, smiling. She was so beautiful. Inside and out. What she had given him in this short amount of time she would never understand. Right now, he found it hard to believe he was terminally ill. He didn't *feel* that way. He felt full of life. And he wanted to celebrate it.

The sun crept into view, filling the vast skies with hues of orange and yellow and pink, diluting the clouds with its warmth and bright rays. It was magnificent!

They watched in awe as it slowly crept upwards in the sky, and he suddenly found himself staring at Bethan, rather than the sun.

She turned her face towards him. 'Thank you.' She smiled. Then kissed him.

And the kiss deepened, becoming something so much more...

CHAPTER SEVEN

'WHAT ON EARTH is that?'

They lay together beneath the blankets in the back of the car, snug and warm, her body wrapped in his. Making love to Cam had been so unexpected! She'd certainly not brought him out here to seduce him or anything. She'd brought him out here to see the sun rise, just as he'd wanted, but watching such beauty form before their eyes had caused them to create their own beauty, so swept up had they been in what they were seeing and feeling.

She'd watched as Cam had stared at the glowing sun, had seen how he had taken in all the colours of the sky. How his face had lit up with a yellow hue as the sun rose. She'd watched him absorb it all, trying to etch it into his memory so that he would always know what it had looked like if he were to lose his eyesight.

It had been such a moving moment, but she'd imagined that once they had seen the sun rise she would bring out her next surprise—the electronic keyboard she had stashed in the back.

She wasn't an expert at the piano by any means—that had been Ashley's forte—but she knew enough to teach Cam something basic. She'd pictured in her mind teaching him the piano as the sun warmed their faces and hands, high on the mountainside above Gilloch.

She flushed. 'Oh, it's surprise number two.'

She watched as he pulled the cover off the keyboard and then laughed at the surprise on his face.

'It's a keyboard,' he said.

She laughed. 'Yes! Well, I could hardly get a grand piano in the back of the car, could I?'

He smiled at her. 'You don't have to give me everything, you know. It doesn't have to be your responsibility.'

'It's not. I'm doing it because I want to.'

He stared back at her, considering her explanation. 'I don't want to use you, Bethan. I don't want you to feel used after all this, when I… when I die.'

'You're not using me… I'm using *you*.'

He gazed at her, confused. 'For what?'

How could she explain? How could she tell him that she was testing herself? Seeing how she felt about getting involved with this man above any other.

She could have had anyone she wanted in this world. A man who wasn't dying. A man who didn't have a time limit, the way Ashley had. A man who wouldn't hurt her by dying and leaving her behind to pick up the pieces.

But she had picked *him*. Because it felt right and because she couldn't imagine being with anyone else. The more she got involved with him, the stronger she knew she was. Even if she was facing death again, having only had him for such a short time.

Perhaps it was the wrong thing to do? She didn't know. But what she *did* know, and what she knew felt *right*, was being in his arms. Being in his embrace and letting her heart have free rein to…*to love him?*

'I need to be with you, Cam. It's as simple as that, right now. I want to give you my all. To show you that love is worth it, even if it is for a short time. Neither of us knows how much time we have, but we know it's limited. Let's embrace every second. Let's enjoy every moment as if it's a sunrise. Let's just be together. I promise you, you won't regret it.'

'But will *you*? Regret it?'

She stroked his face and smiled. 'Never.'

They drove back in silence, occasionally glancing at each other and smiling. Not needing to say anything.

Bethan was right. She did get involved—maybe a bit too quickly—but it wasn't her weakness. It was her strength. She had a resolve and a determination that was unlike most people's.

There were so many people in this world who wouldn't have the strength to care for one dying person, never mind two. Nurses, doctors, first responders—they all had a little extra-special something in their hearts. Caring for those in need was more than just a job. It was a calling.

Something they could not turn away from even if it was to the detriment of themselves. They would always make sure their patient was okay. More than okay, if they could make that happen.

And, even though he hadn't known he wanted it this much, he was extremely glad that she was in his corner. She was a support he hadn't known was missing, and he felt closer to her now than he'd ever believed possible at that first moment she had walked into his surgery.

The sun was rising high now, warming the land, and outside the world was coming to life. No doubt the birds were singing already, and he saw one or two rabbits getting in their last mouthfuls of grass before the car shot past them. He stared at one as they neared it, its little grey furry body curled up as it nibbled at the grass.

As he stared at the rabbit he felt something inside him shift and a hot fork of pain pierced his skull. His hands rushed up to clutch his head. He gasped, the keening sound gushing out of him. Unaware of much except the feel of the hurt deep within his skull, he felt sick, as if he might vomit.

A cold sweat beaded his skin, and then he began to hear her voice.

'Cameron? *Cameron!* What's happening? Speak to me! Please. Tell me what's going on!'

He knew the car had come to a halt, but he couldn't speak. He hurt too much. He was nothing but white-hot pain as the world began to fade out...

'I'm all right now. I feel better.'

Bethan stared at him from the end of his bed, her arms crossed tightly over her body. 'I don't care. You need to stay in bed. Doctor's orders.'

'But I feel fine now. It's gone. It's passed.'

She shone a light into his eyes, checking his pupil reflex. 'Maybe, but you have a little girl in the next room, full of excitement and energy, and you're in no fit state to look after her.'

'I disagree.' He threw back the blankets to get out of bed.

'Don't you *dare* get out of bed, Cameron! Seriously! I'm not joking.' She sounded afraid.

Cameron stopped, his feet on the ground, looking up at her. 'Seriously?'

'Yes. I need to check you over properly.'

'Look, Bethan, I appreciate you're trying to help, but I can call Dr McKellen. I'm sure he can check me over later.'

'What's the point of that when you have a qualified physician in your bedroom already?'

He pulled a face and it made her smile. It was like treating a petulant child. Doctors really did make the worst patients.

'Now, lie back and let me examine you.'

His blood pressure was slightly high—no doubt from the stress—and his pulse was high, too. But nothing that unduly concerned her.

'You really scared me, Cam.'

He looked up at her. 'It scared me, too.'

'Has that happened before? Pain like that out of nowhere?'

'No. It could mean that…' He trailed off, not wanting to finish the thought.

'You think the tumour is advancing? Growing? Possibly. We'd need a scan to confirm. But you can still see? No blurriness?'

'My sight's fine.'

'Honestly?'

He smiled and laid his hand on hers. 'Honestly.'

Bethan looked down at his hand upon hers and she ached for him. Physically felt her heart ache for him. The incident in the car had terrified her. She'd thought she was losing him then and there. When he'd slumped, groaning, clutching his skull as if he wanted to tear off his own head because it hurt so much, she had fought to keep it together. To stay professional and distant when all she'd wanted to scream was, *Don't you die on me, Cameron Brodie! I need you!*

She'd not thought about that again until now. Now that he was no longer in pain and was sitting up in bed, safe in his own home and holding her hand in his.

I need him.

This was so hard! Why was life such a challenge? Just when you thought you had it under control, another crisis would rumble along and tear the ground out from under your feet.

What was she supposed to do? She felt as if she could sit there with his hand on hers for ever, but the idea of seeing him in that much pain again... That was hard. Ashley had been in pain, but he'd had morphine, and it hadn't been in his head—hadn't been as terrifying as what she'd just witnessed with Cam.

The urge to lie down beside him, rest her head upon his chest and just hold him overwhelmed her. She wanted to comfort him. She wanted to feel him against her, to let him know that she would protect him.

Bethan stood up, pulling her hand free from his, her cheeks burning as she went to the window, taking a moment to breathe again.

He's still here. I didn't lose him.

It was a stark reminder of what it had felt like to lose someone she had strong feelings for. Begging for just one more day. One more moment. Not knowing if life would grant her that wish.

Looking out, she saw a vehicle pull up outside. An older man got out, his red hair shot through with grey. This had to be Cam's father.

'Your father's here.'

'I ought to go down and say hi.'

'Stay there. I'll let him know you're up here. He can come to you.'

'Bethan—'

'Please, Cam...do this for me?'

She hurried downstairs and opened the door.

Dougal Brodie gave her a smile. 'The famous Bethan, I take it?'

She smiled. 'How do you do, Mr Brodie?'

He gave her a broad smile and she could see so much of Cam in his father's face. 'I do very well, lass. Even more so since you put my da' in his place.'

Oh. That. Of course. It seems such a long time ago now.

Her cheeks coloured once again.

He laughed—a big, whole-hearted laugh—and stepped forward and gave her a bear hug. 'I've never laughed so much in my entire life hearing him tell the tale!' He let go and looked around. 'How's Cam doing?'

Bethan checked to make sure Rosie wasn't in earshot. 'He's not well.'

The smile disappeared. 'How bad?'

'It was bad.'

She told him in a subdued voice what had happened, and that she was making him rest now, despite his son's protests.

'You're a good 'un, lassie. Need *me* to go up there and tell him to stay in bed, too?'

'If you like—though I think he'll behave.'

'I'll just pop up and see him.'

Bethan waited downstairs and got Rosie a drink and a biscuit from the tin she'd found in the kitchen. Then she put on the television, found a cartoon channel and left it on low in the background while Rosie got out a jigsaw puzzle to solve.

Bethan went into the hall as footsteps came trotting down the stairs once again.

'He's staying put. He knows what's good for him.' Dougal looked at her, his head cocked to one side. 'You're good for this entire family. You put my da' in his place, you're helping Cam and wee Rosie. You're good for us all. You care. I can see it in your eyes. Maybe a bit more than that.'

Bethan wasn't sure what he meant, but she smiled anyway, glad that this Brodie man was happy to see her. Dougal was not her enemy. None of the Brodies had ever been that. It was just a figment of the past, held in the memory of

Angus and Mhairi, who had never quite got over their enforced separation.

'I'll always do my best to look after my patients, Mr Brodie.'

Dougal nodded and opened the front door, ready to go. 'Aye. But he isn't just another patient, though, is he? Bye, Rosie! I'll see you later, lass.' And he waved a goodbye and strolled down the path.

Bethan watched him go, her brain muddled and confused by all that had happened in the last few hours.

As she closed the door she heard her mobile phone ring in the kitchen and she rushed to answer it. Picking it up and glancing at the screen, she saw *Private Number Calling.*

She frowned. Who could it be?

Pressing *Answer*, she lifted the phone to her ear. 'Hello?'

'Bethan? Bethan Monroe? It's Keir MacIntyre.'

Keir. She'd sent him Cameron's scans and reports. He'd been a friend since a long time ago. She'd even had the privilege of watching him operate once, and it had been amazing to watch him work a miracle on a neuroblastoma. The delicateness of his work, the skill involved… He had always seriously impressed her, and she had felt that if there was anyone in the world who could help Cam, it was him.

'Hi. Thanks for getting back to me. Have you had a chance to look at those scans?'

'I have. I'm sorry for the delay in getting back to you, but I wanted to be thorough before I got in touch.'

'And what do you think? Can you help? Is there anything you can do? Anything at all?'

'It's a very difficult tumour, and I'd need a current scan to confirm it hasn't grown too much since this last one, but…yes, I think I can help him.'

She heard the smile in his voice. Heard his confidence. His knowledge and belief in his own skills.

She almost dropped the phone. 'You think you could…' She almost didn't want to jinx things by saying the word *cure*, but that was what he'd suggested. *Right?* 'You could get rid of it? *All* of it?'

'It's an extreme chance. But if the patient is

willing to give it a go then so am I—depending upon the current scan, of course.'

She thought she might faint. She felt hot and dizzy. Her legs weak. She sat down on one of the kitchen chairs, clutching the phone. Cam could *live*! Here was his opportunity to escape his terminal diagnosis!

'When could you do it?'

'As soon as possible. If Mr Brodie is willing to come to Edinburgh, I can dedicate my time to getting him sorted out immediately. We can't wait with this tumour. It's already aggressive. I'm assuming the patient has had no eye infiltration yet?'

'No. He can still see well.'

'That's good to hear. When can you get him to Edinburgh?'

'I don't know. I'll have to tell him first. Can you give me a day or so? So we can organise childcare and travel arrangements?'

'Two days. But no more than that, Bethan. We're risking it as it is.'

'I'll tell him right now. We'll be there.'

'I'll schedule him into my diary.'

* * *

'I'm not doing it.' Cam sat in his bed, staring at her, the muscle in his jaw twitching as he stared straight ahead.

She stared at him, incredulous. 'Did you not hear what I said? He thinks he can get it all out! It would *cure* you!'

'Or kill me. I could die on the table if it goes wrong, or he fails, and I've not had my time with Rosie yet. I promised her I'd be around for a while.'

'But your time with her will not be as you imagine it will. You'll be getting sicker. The tumour will blind you. Does she need to see that happen to you? Do you want to have to explain why you can't see her face any more?'

'That's not fair.'

'Nothing about this *is*! The tumour will make you into a different person, Cam. It's in your *brain*. You'll have mood swings—you might become violent, angry, lash out. I don't mean physically, but verbally. Do you want to put Rosie through that?'

'I would never do that to her. She's not ready for me to die.'

'No child is ever ready when they lose a parent. Even if they know it's coming. Even if they think they've prepared. Even if they're a grown-up themselves. She'll never be ready. Take it from me, Cam, there will never be a *good time* for this. So why not give her a chance to have you for a lot longer? To see her grow up? To see her go off to college, or walk her down the aisle, or introduce you to your grandchildren? You could *have* that.'

'*If* I take the risk.'

'If you take the risk.'

'The window of success is so small… I know nothing about this Keir MacIntyre—he could be a risk-taker.'

'Of *course* he's a risk-taker! He's taking on a tumour that everyone else has said no to. But that's what he does. He gives people who are willing to take the chance an opportunity.'

'To die.'

'To *live*. You're going to die anyway—why not take the chance to stick around for longer than you had ever dreamed?'

Cam shook his head. 'You don't understand…'

Was he *kidding*? He thought she didn't understand how scary this was for him? Or how scary it was for her? She didn't want to lose him either.

'I've just got to have you as my friend, Cam. A truly blessed and great friend. I don't want to lose you. And I don't have to. You've been given a chance to stay, to live—to beat this and stick two fingers up to cancer and gliomas. I need you to be brave enough to do it.'

'Why?'

She didn't want to say why. Didn't want to admit it out loud. But this was life and death, and everything she said here could matter. He needed to know the truth, if he was to make an informed decision.

'Because I care for you. I have feelings for you. And…and I think we could have something amazing if you'll just give it a chance. Give Keir a chance. Look him up on the internet. Research him. Say yes. You'll have to have more scans, but if they're bad, then you won't have lost anything—'

'I *will* lose something.' He looked up at her

with tears in his eyes. 'I'll lose hope. I've accepted my fate. My lot in life, however short it may be. But if I do this it'll make me hope, and I'm not sure I'm strong enough to lose it again. To go all that way? To Edinburgh? With hope in my heart? Do you know how cruel it would be to get turned down when the scan shows the tumour has grown out of control?'

'We don't know that will happen.'

'I know what I felt today. Something's changed. Something bad.'

She nodded and went to sit beside him on the bed, grabbed his hand in hers. 'Yes, something's changed. *We've* changed. What I feel for you—I shouldn't be feeling it, it's too big, it's too scary, but I do.'

Cam gripped her hand and made her look at him. 'I have feelings for you, too. I'd be a terrible liar to deny it. But this—this situation—it's cruel. To give you hope, too. To let you watch me go into surgery, knowing I might die...'

'I'm going to lose you anyway if you don't try. Is *that* fair on me?'

He looked into her eyes with such sadness. 'No. It's not.'

'Nor is it fair on Rosie. But it will happen, Cam. It will. If you don't do something *now* to change it. Please change it. Take action. *Please.*'

Tears ran freely down her cheeks but she didn't care if she had panda eyes—didn't care if she looked awful. He had to know how much this meant. Not just to him, but to her and Rosie and all his family. Everyone who loved him.

Oh...

She gazed into his eyes through blurry tears and he pulled her towards him and kissed her. Just once. A strong, determined kiss.

Then he held her quivering body tight against his, stroking her back. 'Okay. Okay, we'll go.'

CHAPTER EIGHT

'I THINK WE could have something amazing...'

That was what kept going round and round in his mind as they drove to Edinburgh. Alongside the look on his daughter's face as she'd tearfully kissed him goodbye, broken-hearted, hiding behind her grandfather's legs as they drove away.

He knew he should never have turned around for one last look at his family. He'd seen the look in the eyes of his father, seen quite clearly his question—*Is this the last time I'll see my son?*

It had almost been enough to make him turn around and tell Bethan they weren't going.

Almost.

As much as he hated to admit it, since Keir's call he'd thought of nothing else—the possibility that this thing in his head could be taken away completely. That he could be cured...that he could have a life again. A future! With Rosie and those whom he loved.

Bethan.

'I think we could have something amazing.'

So did he. Their connection was strong. Probably because they'd both fought it so much, trying to keep it contained, trying to *deny* it.

When you're told not to think of the elephant in the room, it's all you can do.

Trying not to acknowledge his feelings for Bethan had simply forced him to think of almost nothing else—wondering what might have been, what kind of future they might have had, if only…

And now he had his *if only.* And it was terrifying. Because his chances of dying on the table were high. He could have a rupture, a brain-bleed. He could die. Or wake up in an even worse state, with disabilities he'd never had before *and* a life sentence.

But what if you don't? the voices in his head kept saying. *What if you wake up cured? What if you wake up and it's all gone and you can have everything you've ever wanted?*

This wasn't a fairy tale. There wasn't an imagined pot of gold at the end of the rainbow. This was reality. Keir MacIntyre believed he could do this, so it was possible—no matter how slim the chance.

'How are you feeling?' Bethan asked as she drove them onto the main road out of Gilloch.

'Nauseated. Terrified. You?'

'The same, but hopeful.'

He laid his hand on hers and squeezed. 'Let's not get hopeful yet. I've still got to have the scans, remember? We might see those and then just drive straight back home again.'

She nodded. 'Or they just might give you a bed.'

Cam looked out of the window and let out a big sigh. He hoped so. He hoped that what he'd felt the other day had just been a bad migraine attack and not signs of the tumour encroaching into places he didn't want. It couldn't have grown much—he could still see, after all. His sight had not yet been affected and he'd always assumed the first sign of everything going downhill would be a blurriness of vision, or losing his peripheral vision—something like that.

But for now he could look out at the wondrous landscape that was Scotland. Its high grey mountains, its sweeping valleys filled with gorse and heathers. A pheasant plodded through a field as crows soared high overhead.

Would this be the last time he'd see his beloved country? Were these sights the last things he would ever see? If so, he wanted to soak them up completely. The rich colours—purples, greys, greens. The beautiful blue sky above, with soft, wispy white clouds. The trees in rich brown and chocolate, their silver bark, the shadows beneath them. The broken remains of an old grey stone castle, high on a hilltop.

This was what he wanted to see. Not hospital walls. Not the stark white of an ICU.

'Stop the car.'

'What?'

'Stop the car.'

'Why? You haven't changed your mind, have you? Oh, Cam, please—'

'I haven't changed my mind—just stop the car. I need to do something.'

She checked her mirrors and indicated, pulled over into a small lay-by. She turned to look at him. 'What is it?'

'Get out for a moment.'

He opened his car door and got out, stretching his legs and sucking in a long lungful of air, his gaze on the mountains, aware that Bethan was coming round to his side of the vehicle.

'Do you feel okay?'

He turned to look at her. Beautiful Bethan. *His* beautiful Bethan. He wouldn't be doing any of this if it wasn't for her. He wouldn't have known about this chance to live if it hadn't been for her. He owed it all to her.

'I feel fine. But this could be my last chance to do anything, for all I know, and there's one last thing I want to do before we get embroiled in tests and procedures.'

'What?'

He smiled and took a step towards her, cupping her face with his hands and marvelling at the softness of her skin before bringing her lips to his and kissing her. Just one last time.

Who knew? After this operation he could be dead. He might wake disabled. And if there was one good thing he wanted to lie in bed and remember it was kissing Bethan. Being a man. He might never get the chance to kiss anyone ever again, so right now he wanted to celebrate life.

He'd make love to her if he could, but they were on a main road, not an abandoned mountainside track, and if he was going to make love to this woman again then he wanted it to be wonderful. For both of them. Satin sheets and a four-poster bed. A roaring fire.

He might never get that wish, but he could kiss her. And he was going to kiss her until neither of them could breathe or think of anything else. He wanted everything else in the world to go away, and the only way he could do that was by losing himself. Kissing Bethan was making that happen.

It was all going—the tumour, the possibility of death, the look on Rosie's face as they'd driven away...

Bethan sank into his embrace, kissed him back,

and he only stopped when he felt her tears touch his face.

'Hey, you okay?' He touched his forehead to hers and stared deeply into her eyes.

Traffic roared past beside them, but that didn't matter. All that mattered was her.

'I'm sad.'

'Don't be.'

'I can't help it. Every time you kiss me it makes me think of what we could have.'

He sucked in a breath. 'You think it's going to fail. You think I'm going to die on that table.'

She shook her head. '*No.* I don't want to think that. Not at all. I want this. I want you to have the operation, and I want it to be a success, but the closer we get to Edinburgh, the closer I am to sitting at the bedside of the man that I... I don't want to lose.'

Love. She'd been going to say love.

He'd seen it in her eyes. Her heart. Her soul.

He realised, with a pang, just how emotionally involved she had got with him. How much he meant to her. And he felt guilt. Guilt for putting her in this position. The one thing he'd hoped never to do.

He let out a low sigh and let her go.

She hadn't really known what she was getting into when she'd started all this. Sending off emails to old colleagues, people she'd thought might help. She'd done it once before, when Ashley had got sick, but no one had been able to help him.

This—what was happening now—was all new territory, and she didn't know how to feel. Getting Keir's telephone call had completely thrown her.

She'd hoped so much that someone would be able to help her husband. She'd avidly checked her emails every day. Made secret telephone calls late at night, trying to contact colleagues of colleagues, patiently explaining the situation. And finally she'd had to accept the fact that Ashley was going to die. It had been a weird process of acceptance, of resignation—despite her desire to yell and scream at the world about it being unfair.

Cam was getting a chance. There was hope.

And she didn't know how to feel about that. He could have his scans, go under the knife and die. Within the week!

Am I ready for that?

She had allowed her feelings—*their* feelings—free rein, relishing their connection, the taste and feel of him, drowning in the glory of it, the joy of it, the excitement of it. Finally allowing herself happiness at last—only for it to be threatened like this.

Am I crazy for letting this happen? What's the point if it's all going to end under a surgeon's knife?

Fate was being cruel. Making her go through this again? But it was going to be worth it if he survived! He had a *chance* here. The only way she was going to get through the next few days was to believe in that. With all her heart. Because she had to. There was no other choice.

I love him.

Both families were waiting back home. Waiting for news and updates. She was the one here to support him. The one who would do the hand-holding. The calm, assertive force in the background, the person who had managed this whole event. She would be the one to pace the floor during surgery. She would be the one jumping to her feet every time someone in scrubs walked towards her. She would be the one to make the phone calls home.

Unhelpfully, her mind provided her with a re-run of those moments just after Ashley's death. How she had felt. That empty ache in her heart. The feeling that she couldn't breathe, as if some-one had punched her in the gut. The knowledge that she would never see, hear, speak to or hold her loved one ever again. That he'd left her be-hind.

She'd sworn to never do this again. To get so attached to someone that their death would rip apart her heart. Grace was meant to be her world. And yet here she sat, beside another man with a terminal diagnosis, driving him to a hospital where he might either die on the table or die a few months later, most probably blind and in pain, lashing out at those who cared for him.

The chance of him surviving, of the operation being successful, had to be slim. But it was a chance she believed was worth taking. Because the prize for being brave, the prize for pulling through, would be worth more to her than anything. Because that prize would be love. And a future together.

But what if it all goes wrong? I'm the one who persuaded him to do this. What if he dies? Will his death be on my conscience?

Of course it would. She was playing God when she ought not to be. Trying to save Cam. Pushing her own agenda when it should be his.

A wave of guilt washed over her and she could barely look at him. She felt a wave of heat over her face and let the driver's window down to cool her skin.

'Are you okay?'

She tried to nod enthusiastically. To force a smile. 'Sure!'

If he chose to go ahead it was *his* choice, right? The onus of responsibility was on *him*. Not on her. She couldn't carry guilt about Cam as well as guilt about Ashley. It would be too much.

She risked a glance at him, wishing more than anything that they were in a situation where she could turn this car around and forget everything. Go and watch another sunrise.

'I never did get the chance to teach you the piano.'

'No.'

'Maybe they'll have one in the hospital some-where.'

'You think teaching me "Chopsticks" will im-prove my last few days?'

She smiled. 'You never know.'

'Well, we still might get sent home, once Keir has seen the scans. Perhaps you can teach me then?'

She didn't want to blurt out, *But what if you don't get sent home? What if you stay and they operate and it all goes wrong?*

'Let's just get there and do the scans. See what they say. Whatever you decide, I'll back you one hundred per cent.'

But even as she said it she knew she was lying. She was trying to make *him* make the decision—the final decision—because then it would be off her shoulders. The responsibility would be his.

But if Keir thought he could operate and Cam

walked away she had no idea how she'd feel. She would always wonder in the days to follow, as she watched Cam deteriorate and then pass away, if he might have survived? If he might have had a life. She would feel so much anger towards him if he walked away from that chance.

She didn't want to hate him.

She wanted to love him. So very much!

And that was what made everything so difficult.

The Royal Livingston Hospital sat atop a hill—a crowning glory of glass and steel, looking down upon the city below.

Bethan drove around the car park twice before they found a parking spot, and Cameron couldn't help but fear that this was some kind of omen— *There's no space for you here. Go home.*

Once they were parked, they headed inside and got directions up to Keir's office in the neurosurgical department. A prim receptionist with thickly curled silver hair asked them to take a seat and they sat nervously in the waiting room, staring at an abstract painting of a brain that was actually made out of carefully folded naked people.

They didn't speak. Neither seemed to have anything to say. He knew that they were both waiting to see what Keir said. What the scans said. There was nothing else either of them could do. As doctors, they wanted the science and the evidence before them. It seemed silly to talk over hypotheticals now.

Cam felt sick. Nervous. He wished he was back home in Gilloch with Rosie, reading her a story or doing something that was absolutely nothing to do with life or death. Looking out of his cottage window at the moorland beyond, trying to spot a partridge or a pheasant or a deer. He'd never liked big cities. Had never liked their impersonal touch—

'Dr Brodie?'

A man stood facing him, dressed in a suit, shirt and tie, a stethoscope draped casually around his neck and an ID card clipped to his belt. This had to be Keir MacIntyre, and Cam was briefly reassured that he looked to be in his mid-forties, experienced and knowledgeable, rather than like someone fresh out of medical school.

He managed a smile and shook Keir's hand, then he and Bethan followed him into his consulting room.

'Please, take a seat. Bethan, it's good to see you—you're looking well.'

He watched, detached, as Keir kissed Bethan's cheek and briefly considered what a handsome couple they would make after his death.

'Thank you for seeing us, Keir.'

'No problem. I had a good long look at those scans you sent me—and the medical history. That's one hell of a glioma you've got here, Dr Brodie.'

'Cam, please. And, yes, it is. But you think you can do something about it?'

Keir nodded. 'As long as the scans are good, and it hasn't grown past its margins from the last one, I think so. I think there's a chance.'

'How much of a chance?' Cam asked, needing to know numbers. Percentages. Risk levels.

'I couldn't possibly say until we get you scanned.

I've blocked some time on the scanner for eleven o'clock, if you're all ready to go?'

This was it, then. Cam nodded, not trusting himself to speak. Being back inside these hospital walls reminded him of having chemo. He'd always hated being a patient, and he hated it even more now. It was such a surreal conversation—discussing whether you'd live out the week or not.

Keir smiled. 'First things first, though…'

He ran Cam through some of the finer details of his medical history—first sign of symptoms, type of symptoms, medication he was on, family medical history—all the things he already had in front of him on his computer, but he was clearly double-checking.

'Any recent new symptoms?'

'No, nothing—'

'He had a head pain,' interrupted Bethan. 'The day you called us. Just before your call, actually. He seemed fine. We were in the car, driving home, and then he screamed and bent double, clutching his head.'

'But I was fine afterwards. It only lasted a few seconds,' Cam explained.

'But it happened.' Bethan's face was serious. She was determined to make sure Keir had all the facts. Was she trying to jeopardise the operation? Perhaps *she* was having second thoughts about the operation? Despite being the one to push for it? He felt a frisson of irritation.

'And, yes, it did pass—but it was the worst I'd seen him.'

'Okay, that's good to know. Well, if you're ready, then, Cam, I'll call a nurse to take you down to the Imaging Centre and we'll get straight to work.'

'Okay.'

This was it. This moment—or rather, the next hour or so—would determine whether he lived a long and happy life, or whether he died, as expected, in his own bed in just a few months.

He almost couldn't feel his legs. Would they work at all? His stomach was working overtime—his acid production seemed to be in overdrive, churning up his guts. He pushed up from the chair and found he could stand, and walk, too.

A nurse met him at the door and he followed

her to the Imaging Centre, got dressed in a blue hospital gown and lay down on the machine's bed.

She passed him the panic button, popped a pillow under his knees and then clamped down the cage over his face. There was a small mirror inside it, so that he could see the technicians in another room.

He felt incredibly alone. And insignificant. Not worth all this trouble. Surely the scan would just show that his glioma—his *aggressive* glioma— had done nothing but grow. Invading his brain… Tendrils of tumour snaking through so many areas it would be impossible to contain it…

Keir would take a look and see an impossible job. He would send Cameron and Bethan home. One to die and one to cry.

Why am I putting everyone through this?

He'd never wanted to involve Bethan. *Ever.* And yet he'd given her permission to send out his scans, his medical history, he'd kissed her, held her in his arms, made love to her and let her drive him here. His only support.

She would be the one to hold his hand as he heard the bad news, and she would have to drive him home to die. Or she would have to sit in a cold, sterile waiting room, staring at the clock for hours, waiting for news. News that would most likely be dire.

He couldn't do this to her. It wasn't fair. On either of them. He'd let her become involved far too much. He had to stop it.

As the machine began to hum all around him he vowed he would send her home as soon as the scans were done. Somehow he would get her to leave.

Let a nurse call home with bad news. Or Keir could do it.

He'd taken this too far with Bethan, and it was only now, as he lay prone in the scanner that hummed and clanked all around him, minutely scanning the layers of his brain, that he could see where all his mistakes lay.

He'd been selfish. He had allowed his need for comfort and love to get in the way of what he knew was the logical thing to do.

* * *

'How did it go? The scan?' she asked Cam as he came out of the changing room after getting back into his clothes.

He said nothing. Just shrugged.

'Did the technicians give you any clue?'

She was hungry for news and didn't understand why he wasn't saying anything. Maybe he was just scared.

Cam sat down in the waiting room and stared into space.

This cold shoulder she was feeling from him was unsettling. What was going on?

'Cam?'

Nothing.

'Will you answer me?'

Finally he turned, stared at her with coldness and detachment in his eyes. 'I want you to go back to Gilloch. Just go and…and forget about me.'

She laughed, incredulous. 'Oh, it's that easy, is it? What kind of world do you live in that people can just wash their hands of each other?'

'I'm serious, Bethan. I should never have got you involved in all this. I want you to go.'

She crossed her arms. 'Well, I'm not going.'

'I can tell Keir I don't want you here and he'll make you leave, but I'd rather you did it yourself.'

She watched him as he continued to button up his shirt. The scan was over. He'd been in that machine for almost forty-five minutes and it had been forty-five minutes of hell for her. What would it show? Did he still have a chance? Would Keir take the risk and try to save him?

'I can't leave you alone. You'll have no one here to support you.'

'I don't need support.'

'If you have brain surgery you will.'

And then a thought entered her head. A frightening realisation.

'You're not going to do it, are you? No matter what he says, you're backing out.'

'Oh, I'll do it. If there's a chance for me, then I'm going to do it.'

'I'm glad to hear it. But why do you want me to go?'

He turned, then. Glared at her. 'Because I should

never have involved you! I knew it was wrong.
From the very first day we met I told myself I
wouldn't even *tell* you what was going on and I
couldn't even get that part right.'

'Your grandfather let the cat out of the bag.
Not you.'

She couldn't believe what she was hearing. He
wanted her to go? Did he really think that she
could do such a thing?

He turned away. 'After all you've been through…'

'Which is on *my* shoulders, not yours.'

'After all you've been through I need to do this
next part right and I need to do it on my own. You
shouldn't have to take responsibility for me—this
shouldn't be your job.'

She stared at him, not quite believing her ears.
'You don't get it, do you?'

He stared at her.

'You're not a *job*, Cam. You're a person I care
about. A great deal. Probably more than I should,
yes, but I do so willingly. I'm a grown woman
and I'm old enough to make my own choices. I
choose to be here to support you, no matter what.'

She saw tears fill his eyes. Tears he tried to blink away.

Bethan took his hand. 'Tell me what you're feeling.'

But he pulled his hand free, sending the pain of hurt and rejection through her chest.

'I just don't think we should ever have got involved with each other. It was a bad idea from the start.'

She shook her head. He was wrong. They were destined to be involved. 'Let me be here for you, Cam. Don't be alone. No one should be alone in something like this.'

He looked up at her, meeting her gaze with tear-filled eyes. He was looking for something— something inside her that only he knew. Whatever it was, he seemed to find it. Or at least he found the answer he was looking for.

She could hardly believe that this was the same man who had made her stop the car so that he could kiss her. That within the space of a few hours he had changed completely.

He turned away from her, crossed his arms, his voice brooking no argument. 'I need you to go.'

* * *

He watched her bottom lip begin to tremble.

'I can't…' she whispered.

It was killing him, seeing her like this. So small. So broken. But it had to be done if he was going to save her from having to sit by his bedside. From being the one to hear from Keir whether the operation had been successful.

If he'd thought about this more clearly he would have left her back at Gilloch and had his father drive him in instead.

'I'm going in to see Keir on my own. I'll hear the results alone. Make my decision alone.'

'Make your decision? But you've already said you're going to have the operation if it's possible—'

'If it's possible, I want to do it alone. I won't have you sitting by my bed, waiting for me to wake up. I won't have you nursing me. I won't have you being the one to ring my family if it all goes wrong!'

He wanted her to remember him as a vital, strong man. The man with whom she'd watched a sunrise. The man with whom she'd made love—

such a cherished memory for him. The man who had held her in his arms, strong and vibrant, keeping her safe.

'Then why bring me in the first place?' Her voice trembled as tears trickled down her cheeks.

'I made a mistake.'

He had to turn away. Couldn't bear to see the pain in her eyes, the hurt she was feeling at his rejection. But he simply couldn't think of any other way to protect her from what was to come.

He had no idea what the scans would say, but he knew in his heart that he was going to tell Keir to try anyway. Even if he only got *some* of the tumour it would be better than nothing. It might buy him some more time with his daughter. He would have liked more time with Bethan, too, but he could see now how wrong it had been for him to get involved with her. To put her through such a thing when she had already faced it once.

The sand in his hourglass was finite. He had less than everyone else. He should have remembered that. But that desire, that yearning to fall in love, had overwhelmed everything the second she had walked into his life. Given him warmth and brightness. He'd known it back then, on the first day they'd met, that she would be more than just a colleague. More than just a woman to replace him. There'd been a connection from the very first second.

And he'd allowed it to happen—succumbing to its potent force, giving in to its temptation. Unable to fight it because he'd wanted it so much.

And now I love her. And I'm hurting her. But I'm doing it to save her. She'll thank me. One day.

'I can't believe this. That you're saying this now. This isn't you, Cam. It's fear speaking. *I* know it. *You* know it.'

'It doesn't matter. I just know I have to do what's right.' He turned back to face her. 'I don't love you, Bethan. You should go.'

'Is Bethan not joining us?' Keir asked as he invited Cameron back into his office.

Cam had been staring at that image of the human brain for far too long, trying not to let the tears fall, trying to identify the separate bodies, the separate shapes that made up the whole.

Because that was the only way he wasn't going to fall apart at suddenly being alone.

'She...er...got called back home,' he lied.

He had no idea if she'd gone home or not. All he'd seen was the way she'd picked up her handbag and run from him, crying.

Keir frowned as he sat down and rubbed his jawline. 'There's no way she can come back?'

No. Definitely not. She's long gone, I made sure of that.

Cam leaned forward. 'Why would she need to come back?'

'Because you'll need someone here when you come round from the operation.'

Cam let out a slow, steady breath as the import of Keir's words sank in. *'Because you'll need someone...'*

All other thoughts, all his guilt, disappeared. 'You can do it?'

The other man smiled. 'I think I can. I'll need another detailed scan to confirm, of course, but the first signs are promising.'

'You can take it out?'

'Clean margins. Yes.'

Cam exhaled, long and steady, once again. 'What's the chance of success?'

'I'm not keen to discuss numbers like those. There are all types of risk factors with deep brain surgery—unexpected bleeding, a rise in pressure, cardiac factors...'

'I need a number.'

Keir looked at him, unblinking. 'I think we're looking at a thirty per cent chance of success.'

Thirty per cent? That was almost nothing. 'So a seventy percent chance of failure?'

'Or the operation could be a success but you may be left with...deficits.'

'Such as?'

'We wouldn't know until you woke up.'

'*If* I woke up.'

Keir nodded. 'This is why you need someone here with you. You need to discuss this with someone you trust before you make such a big decision. I know Bethan. She can handle this.'

'I've already made my decision. I made it before I came here.'

'And that is?'

'To give myself a chance of a life. I have to do it. For my daughter.'

It can't be for Bethan any more. I've ruined that. But I had to do it to save her.

'How old is she?'

'Five.'

'I have a ten-year-old. A boy.'

'So you understand why I have to do this?'

Keir stared at him for a moment. Then nodded. 'I do. I just wish you weren't doing it alone.'

Cam stared back at the consultant. He wouldn't understand why. No matter how much he tried to explain.

They're going to operate. I have a chance. And so does Bethan.

He was in a hospital gown. In a hospital bed. He would have his operation first thing tomorrow.

Around him in the six-bed ward it was visiting time, and he was the only person without a friend or family member at his side. He'd called home already. Told them the operation was a go and that he was going to do it. His father had offered to bring Rosie before he went down to Theatre, but Cam didn't want to think of her waiting for him to come out of surgery.

If he made it out of surgery.

And Bethan? Where was she now? If he died on the table tomorrow all she would remember would be his rejection of her. Telling her he didn't love her.

He'd lied. Of *course* he'd lied! But he was trying to protect her—and if she was angry with him…well, that was better than being desolate with grief, wasn't it?

He hadn't meant it. But he couldn't put her through the waiting game. Couldn't make her be the one to have to drive home and tell his family either that he had died or had woken with deficits.

He could remember driving home to tell everyone that Holly had died. He could remember telephoning Holly's parents with the news of Rosie's birth—giving them the good news first, hoping to give them that one ray of sunshine before telling them the rest—and the silence down the phone that had seemed to last an age. And then that terrible wailing sound her mother had made. The crying. The anguish.

He'd sat on the other end of the phone, feeling powerless and just as devastated himself, not knowing what to do, knowing that they would remember him only as the man who had told them their daughter had died.

He couldn't allow people to think of Bethan that way. He didn't want her blamed for anything. She had given him this gift. This chance to save his life. This attempt to give him back everything he needed—time.

And what if he woke with deficits? Such a politically correct word. Less frightening than blindness, or the inability to speak or to feed yourself. Less daunting. Smaller somehow. Less frightening.

Or was it?

He hoped the operation would be a success. Of course he did. He'd looked up Keir's record and his results were fifty-fifty. But, then again, he did take on the cases that no one else would, so fifty-fifty was quite impressive when you considered that. Cam trusted Keir's ability in Theatre.

Hopefully Bethan would forgive him. She

would realise why he had said what he had. That he'd been doing it to save her. To help her.

If only I could forget the look on her face just before she left...

Cam didn't sleep well, and the night was long and uncomfortable. At last the ward lights were being switched on and everyone was served breakfast except him. He got a pre-med instead. And a blood pressure check.

One last phone call with Rosie... She sounded happy to hear his voice, and he could picture her at home in his father's kitchen, sat upon his knee as she ate her porridge, topped with honey just as she liked it.

'Have you spoken to Bethan?' he asked his father.

'Bethan? No. Isn't she with you?' his dad asked, sounding confused.

'No, she, er ...' and then he ran out of words. Didn't know how he could explain it to his father. What he had done to Bethan. What he had said.

There was another silence then, for a few seconds. 'I love you, son. And I'm so proud of you for doing this. I know the chances are small, but the fact that you're taking that chance… Well, I'm very proud of you.'

He heard the crack in his dad's voice. Normally he was a man so stoic he'd give statues a run for their money.

'Thanks, Dad. I love you, too.'

He wished he'd been brave enough to say that to Bethan.

Bethan stood watching at the far end of the corridor as Cam was prepped and taken to Theatre. She felt sick to her stomach as the nurses began to wheel him out in his bed, wishing she could run up to him one last time and hold him. Kiss him.

She watched, following silently behind them, as they walked down the corridors towards Theatre, then stopped behind the red line as he disappeared through a set of double doors.

Fear kept her silent.

She glanced up at the big wall clock and noted the time. How long would this take? When would she know? When would her heart break?

Keir noticed her and came over. 'It's good to see you. You've got a long wait ahead of you.

Why don't you get something to eat? Maybe get some rest?'

'I don't think I could eat a thing.'

He nodded, understanding. 'I'll look after him. I'll do my best for him.'

She braved a smile. 'I know you will.'

Keir gave her a brief hug. 'I ought to go.'

Bethan nodded, feeling tears prick her eyes. 'Do your best work in there. For Cameron.'

'I will.'

Cam lay in Theatre and wondered if this room was the last thing he would ever see in his life. He hoped not.

He'd always imagined that he would die in his bed at home. Surrounded by family. Holding their hands. Looking into the eyes of his daughter. Or Bethan. Either one of those would have been good. But he knew he'd burnt his bridges with Bethan. He'd had to be cruel to be kind—she'd work that out in the end.

The mask was lowered over his face and he began to count back from ten as in his mind's eye he pictured their last kiss. Tried to remember the feel of her in his arms.

If he was going to die now, he wanted to die happy.

CHAPTER NINE

'ANY NEWS?' NANNA asked over the telephone.

Bethan glanced at the clock. Cam had been under the knife for almost five hours so far. An interminable amount of time. Especially since she knew she had gone against his final wishes. If he died…

'No, nothing yet.'

She'd needed to hear a kind voice. A comforting voice. To talk to someone who wouldn't blame her, or try to interpret what she had done. There would be no judgement from Nanna.

'You'd think these doctors would know that people are waiting and worrying. Would it hurt them to come out and tell you occasionally that it's all going okay?'

'I'd rather they were in there worrying about him, not me.'

'Of course. You're right. Grace is here. Do you want to have a quick chat?'

Yes. She did. More than anything right now she wanted to hear her daughter's bright, happy tones. The voice of someone who loved her and valued her.

Cameron had crushed her with his admission that he didn't love her. She'd thought that maybe he did. She'd thought that perhaps he felt the same way as her.

So what if he didn't? It didn't mean that she had to stop caring about him. She could never leave him at a time like this, no matter what he'd said. He could have said *I hate you* and she would not have walked away. What did that say about her? That she was stupid? Stubborn? A glutton for punishment?

She didn't care. She just needed to know in her own heart that she had done the right thing. If the operation worked and Cameron lived through it she would do the decent thing and walk away. Leave him to his life with Rosie. She would be polite, but distant, and only she would know the turmoil that was in her heart. She would not let him see anything.

And if he died…

You won't have died alone.

She almost choked on a sob at the thought, and had to pretend to Grace that she was just clearing her throat. Grace babbled on, utterly unaware of her mother's anguish.

What Keir managed to do in that room would either end everything or give Cameron everything he'd ever wanted. She hoped, for his sake, it was the latter. And if it was successful she would make sure he was okay and *then* she would leave. It would be the right thing to do. She and Grace and Nanna would carry on looking after themselves, keeping their noses out of anything to do with Cameron, and hopefully live in peace together within the confines of Gilloch village.

Grace chattered on about what she'd got up to at school that day, and how Nanna had allowed her to invite Rosie to their house for a playdate and sleepover.

Bethan's heart sank at the thought of the budding friendship between the two girls. If the surgery worked, she would have to decide the best way to deal with it. Maybe let them remain friends, but put the stop on playdates and parties and sleepovers. She didn't want to have to see Cameron if she could help it. It would hurt too much. Or maybe she'd let them happen and Nanna could take Rosie back to her father's house each time. Why should the girls suffer just because their parents couldn't get it together?

But the thought of having to be indifferent almost broke her heart in two. Her feelings for him had grown exponentially. They were unstoppable and he had hurt her unbearably.

When Nanna got back on the phone, Bethan asked, 'How is Rosie? Has she said anything about her father?'

'Just that he's in hospital. She seems to think he'll be coming home soon. I daren't say anything, just in case.'

'No, it's best not to. I'll ring when I have news.'

'Have you eaten? Are you looking after yourself?'

'I've got a sandwich,' she lied, staring at the

cold cup of coffee that sat before her on the low table.

'Good. You need to keep your strength up. I hope it's successful for him, I really do, but I'll be a lot happier when you're back home safe and sound with me.'

'Me, too.'

It was the truth. All she wanted was to be surrounded by love once again. To sink into the loving warmth of her nanna's embrace and try to forget that her heart belonged to Cameron.

The next few hours passed slowly. She couldn't eat. Or drink. She just sat and watched the clock tick round and round. And then, after twelve hours and forty-two minutes of surgery, she saw Keir walking towards her.

He still wore scrubs. He looked tired, but beyond that she wasn't sure of his expression. His face gave nothing away.

It was only when he stood in front of her and she got up from her chair and asked, 'Well…?' that he began to smile. Broadly.

'I got it. I got it all.'

'You got the tumour?' She almost didn't believe it.

'Yes. It's all up to him now. He's got a long future ahead of him with you by his side.'

As Keir walked away she sank back into her chair. Cameron was going to be okay! Well, he'd made it out of surgery, at least. Whether he'd suffered any deficits was yet to be known, but he would *live*.

I can go home now.

But her feet wouldn't move. She knew she couldn't go. She had to be there when he woke up.

'With you by his side...'

Her heart thundered away in her chest.

I have to make sure he's okay.

She sat in the neurological intensive care unit beside his bed, waiting for him to wake. Afraid of his judgement when he did. But she had *some* pride. She would not cry. She would not beg. She would just tell him that he was okay. That it was over. And then she would leave.

The nurse had said he'd briefly come round

after the operation, mumbled something she couldn't understand and then gone back to sleep again.

'His body has been through an ordeal. He needs to rest. We'll know more later,' she'd said, hoping to be reassuring.

Bethan didn't need to be reassured. What she needed was to steel herself for seeing him open his eyes, telling him he'd made it through.

She could not be with him. A man who had told her to her face that he didn't love her. Had he used her? Maybe. She was too confused to know anything for sure right now.

She should never have got involved with Cameron Brodie. She should have listened to Nanna.

Cam stirred and her gaze instantly latched onto his face to see if he was about to open his eyes. His head was wrapped in a bandage, and he looked so pale, but all the machines around him were beeping out a reassuring rhythm. Numbers…measurements that she knew she could trust.

His heart-rate seemed good. His blood pressure was stable. Inter-cranial pressure exactly what it should be. No temperature spikes. He just needed to wake. She just needed to see that he wasn't blind, that he wasn't deaf and that he could talk—that was all she needed to know.

She wanted to give him the comfort of not waking alone and then she would go. It would hurt to walk away, but she would do it. It wasn't safe for her to stay—because if she stayed she would continue to love him, and she couldn't allow herself to do that.

He moaned. Muttered something unintelligible.

She felt her mouth go dry. He looked so helpless in the bed. She yearned to reach out and stroke his brow. Run her fingers along his bearded jaw. Tell him that she loved him. That she wished him all the best. A happy future with Rosie. And that she would no doubt see him out and about in the village, but that would be all.

They would be like strangers. Strangers who might have been something more.

His eyes fluttered open, blinking in the bright lights of the intensive care unit.

He can see.

Light, at least. Could he see anything more? Shapes? Faces? Details?

'Bethan?'

She gasped upon hearing her name spoken from his lips.

He can talk!

And his first word had been her name!

Don't get excited. It doesn't mean anything.

Fighting the urge to rush to his bedside and cover his face with grateful kisses, she stood stiffly, away from the bed, gritting her teeth, determined not to move her feet. Had he the right to ask for her after the way he'd dismissed her before?

'I'm here, Cameron.'

His head turned towards her voice.

He can move. He can hear.

And his eyes were focused upon her face.

'You're here.'

'I had to make sure you were okay.'

His gaze travelled around the room, taking in his surroundings, the machines he was hooked up to, then moved back to her face once again. 'Is it over?'

Yes. It's all over.

'Yes. Keir did it. He got the tumour. You're going to be fine.'

He frowned as he listened to her, but said nothing as he processed the immensity of her news. A ghostly smile lifted the corners of his mouth. 'I'll live?'

'A long time. You have a future, now.'

Without me.

'But I... Does everyone...?'

He was tired. His sentences were falling away before he could complete them. It was understandable—and expected.

'I'll call everyone. Let them know.'

His gaze fell back to her face. Studied her. 'Why do you seem so sad?'

She gazed down upon him, feeling a wearying sadness exhausting her body. They'd both been through so much in the last day or two. She was spent, too. And it was hard work, shutting down her heart. Telling it that it could no longer have feelings for the man she had come to love. She'd done it once before and survived.

I can do it again.

It hurt. And it was terrifyingly familiar. Like a death. Only worse. The man of her heart still lived. He was still here. And she would see him every day. Be reminded of what she had lost every day.

Perhaps it would have been better if she had never returned to Gilloch? Perhaps she should be thinking of moving away again? Only it wasn't that simple. She was a doctor now. She had taken on the post at Gilloch promising that she would stay.

But he won't need me there any more. He's survived. He's going to live. He can be a doctor once again, setting me free.

The thought did not cheer her in the least.

'I have to go now. I just needed to make sure you were okay. You were right, Cameron. I'm walking away because you don't need me any more. Perhaps you never did. I thought you were safe. Can you believe that? That your diagnosis made me safe. I thought I wouldn't be risking my heart with you. Only I did. I'm sorry.'

And she turned on her heel and walked away. She heard him try to call out. To stop her, perhaps? But all it succeeded in doing was making hot, salty tears fall from her eyes.

Cam had never needed her except as someone to step into his shoes when he'd believed he was on his way out through the exit door of life. Only he'd been given a reprieve. A last-minute chance.

No one except maybe Nanna needed her to stick around any more. Cameron could have his old job back. Everything could return to how it was before.

Perhaps I should stay for Nanna.

But something inside her told her that that was all she ever did. Fitted her life around other people's needs. When had she ever put her own needs first? She hadn't with Ashley. She hadn't with Cam. Not until now. Would Nanna want her to stay because of her? Surely she would see how unhappy she was and tell her to go and make her own life for once?

She'd thought she'd already done it—by returning to Gilloch. But she'd been wrong. So terribly wrong. And it had taken Cameron's second chance at life to make her see that maybe she needed to give *herself* a second chance at a life.

She pressed the button to open the door and walked out, knowing that this time she would drive away. There was no need for her to return.

Every step was a stab in her heart. Every movement away from him, from her heart, her soul, tore her in two. Tears streamed down her face as she fought to breathe, as she fought to keep her back straight and not crumple into a heap on the ground.

Cameron didn't need her. He didn't want her. He didn't love her the way that she loved him.

Now she was putting herself first.

And it was time to go home to her daughter and live.

'It was *so* good to see Dr Brodie!' Janet enthused, clutching her mug of hot, steaming tea. 'Smiling and chatting away like he hadn't a care in the world! It really was quite naughty of him to keep the fact that he was still ill from everyone. Especially when he must have known how concerned we were about him.'

Bethan nodded and smiled. She'd bet he didn't have a care in the world. He was healthy again.

No terminal diagnosis any more. A future with his daughter. Which was all that he'd wanted.

The last week for her had been the complete opposite, but no one apart from Nanna had seen it in her eyes.

'I called in on him yesterday morning,' Janet went on. 'He comes home from the hospital late on Monday, by all accounts.'

Bethan smiled. 'That's great.'

Next week? That meant she only had a few more days before she might start seeing him around. That was going to be hard. She wasn't sure she was ready yet. Everything was still so raw.

'I've booked him onto the system so that you can give him a home check.'

Bethan blinked. 'Sorry? What did you say?'

'I've booked him in for a home visit. Early Tuesday morning—he's your first patient.'

'He's not a patient at this surgery—he's booked in under Dr McKellen in the next village.'

'Och, I know, lass, but Dr McKellen is away for two days at a conference, and Dr Brodie has to have a doctor's visit on his return home. It's one of the conditions of his release. I knew you wouldn't mind, what with the two of you being such firm friends.'

Her heart was racing. Thudding away in her chest like a pneumatic drill. Of *course* she minded! Having to see him. Touch him. Speak to him!

She suddenly felt a bit faint and sat down in her chair.

'Are you okay, lass? You've gone awful pale.'

'Oh, just…er…low blood sugar. I'll have something to eat.'

She grabbed a chocolate digestive from the packet on the table, but it was like ash in her mouth. Like chewing wood shavings. She felt sick, but she forced the biscuit down and sipped at her tea to help it on its way.

'I'd better get the day started.' She hurried away before Janet made her explain anything.

Cameron's going to be my patient?

Was it too late to quit? Would people think badly of her if she just turned tail and ran? Of course they would.

And I'm meant to be made of sterner stuff than

this! I'll just have to be polite. Quick. Check him over and leave. Hopefully he'll be surrounded by the entire Brodie mob and we won't have any chance to talk.

Her first patient of the day was Malcolm McDowd. He shuffled into the room, looking tired and exhausted, leaning on his walking stick heavily and sinking into the chair with a sigh.

'Morning, Doctor.'

'How can I help you today?' She desperately wanted a conversation that didn't concern Cameron. Just for a short while it would be nice not to have to think about him at all.

Malcolm sighed again. 'I don't know why I'm here, really. I guess I just need someone to talk to. Someone who'll understand.'

Bethan glanced at his medical records on screen. Malcolm suffered from type two diabetes and high blood pressure. He had a bad hip after a car accident many years ago, and he was also a carer for his wife, who had Alzheimer's.

'Things have been a bit difficult lately with Barbara. She doesn't know who she is half the time, or where she is, and she keeps getting

scared. Screams half the night. I get no sleep—I
have to keep going in to reassure her. And when
she's not scared, she's yelling at me. Throwing
things. See this mark here?' He pointed at a small
cut just above his left eye. 'That was a cup. Nothing hot in it, though, thank God.'

'It must be difficult for you. Do you get any
respite?'

He shook his head. 'No. She made me promise. I swore to her that I…' He sniffed and wiped
at his nostrils with a proper cotton handkerchief.
'But I guess now she doesn't even know who I
am, so getting someone in might help.'

'I can certainly make some arrangements for
you to be assessed, Malcolm. Carers today are
hugely recognised for the contribution they make,
and everyone is aware of how the carers themselves need time off. Perhaps we could get someone in to do the mornings and evenings for you?
You know…getting her up and dressed, and then
put back into bed again at night?'

'I'd feel so bad about not doing it myself. Like
I'm letting her down.'

She knew all about feeling as if she'd let some-one down...

'You're not, though. By looking after yourself you're helping her in the long run. Have you any other family that could help? Maybe give you a weekend away occasionally?'

'Our daughter down in Newcastle might—but she's got kiddies of her own to care for.'

'Sometimes people don't realise you need help if you don't ask for it. They assume you're okay because you put on a brave face for them. It's okay to hold your hands up and say you need a break. Some time for *you*.'

'Well, if you could arrange anything, Doctor, that would help me. It'd be nice to get down the bowling green once again—I do miss my games.'

She smiled. 'I bet. I'll send off a letter and I'll also give the respite teams a call. See what they can do at short notice. You're happy for me to give them your contact details—phone number, that kind of thing?'

Malcolm nodded. 'It's a weight off my mind. Thank you, Doctor. I hate to ask. No one likes to show weakness, do they?'

No. They didn't. If *she* ever did she quickly made up for it. She liked to think she used her fear in a positive way—unlike Cameron, who used his in a negative way. At least that was how she was explaining his actions—he'd been scared. But people often revealed their true selves when they were afraid. Saying what they really felt— and Cameron had been blunt and to the point.

'I don't love you, Bethan.'

'Let's check your blood pressure whilst you're here.'

She grabbed the cuff and wrapped it around Malcolm's upper arm, then manually pumped up the sleeve, listening in with her stethoscope, waiting to hear the pulsations that would give her his systolic and diastolic readings.

She released the cuff from his arms and smiled. 'It's a little high, still. One forty-two over ninety-six. But not as bad as it was before, so it's going in the right direction. Are you still taking your medication?'

'Yes, Doctor.'

'And your statins?'

'Every day—regular as clockwork.'

'Good. Barbara needs you to look after your-self.'

'And who's looking after *you*?' he asked, with a slightly cheeky grin. 'Young slip of a thing like you?'

She smiled politely. 'No one. But I like it that way.'

'You must miss it—being married. I heard you were a widow. I'm so sorry, lass. I can't imag-ine not having my Barbara—even if she doesn't know who I am. I know who *she* is, though.'

There was so much she missed. The easy nature of just being with someone every day. Having someone to hold you tight. Having someone you could talk to. Nanna did her best, but it wasn't the same. And she missed Cameron. Missed feeling loved by him.

I was so convinced he loved me, too! But per-haps it was all just on my side.

Relationships were complicated, and they often caused more pain than you needed.

'I miss some things, but not all.'

Malcolm struggled to his feet. 'No, I understand that, lass. People are hard, but I find that in the end the difficulties are worth it.'

'You think so?' she asked him as he ambled towards the door.

She tried to work out if her difficulties with Cameron had been worth it. She didn't think so. All she'd been left with was hurt and loneliness. She'd felt fine before she got involved with him!

'If you love them, yes. My Barbara doesn't know who I am, but I know who *she* is and that's what matters. Her brain may not recognise me, but my heart recognises her, and no matter how hard you may try you can't just shut those things down. Except maybe with some heavy medication.'

He smiled.

'Thank you, Doctor. For today. For listening. It's been such a long time since anyone's actually heard what I've been saying. I don't get many visitors.'

'You take care of yourself.'

She smiled back at Malcolm as he left, but she was left feeling empty. It had been a long time since anyone had heard *her*, too. She did try to say what she felt, but she always got shot down. Nanna did it sometimes. Grace often did—but she was just a child. And Cameron. Had *he* ever listened to what she had to say? What she felt?

He'd said his piece in the hospital and it had stunned her into silence. But had she ever been given *her* chance to speak? To say what *she* needed to say?

Perhaps that was why she still felt so bad? Because she hadn't been given any closure? Given her chance, her moment, to say what Cameron had meant to her?

Should she say anything on Tuesday at his home visit? Or would that be unprofessional?

All she knew was that her heart *ached*. It physically hurt in her chest. Every morning since she'd left the hospital in Edinburgh she'd woken with no energy whatsoever. Each day was like wading through molasses.

And as for the idea of seeing him again... She wanted to—so much! But then again she was scared to. Seeing him again would open up the wound.

She could never *un*-hear what he had said to

her. Would he remember? Or would he have forgotten it now? Was he concentrating only on his
recovery? Thinking only of how he could get
back to full strength the quickest? He was surrounded by his family, with his little girl, imagining the future they now had together.

She had provided him with that gift. At least
she had contributed to making it happen. Was he
headache-free for the first time in a long time?
Bethan imagined that he was probably the happiest man on the planet right now...

In the quiet of the nights he remembered how
she'd walked away from him. And how he'd
wanted to stop her. In what should have been
one of the happiest moments of his life she had
changed everything, and in his exhaustion, and
the fugue after the anaesthetic, chained to the
bed by monitoring equipment and IVs, he had
felt himself slipping away back into sleep when
all he'd wanted to do was run after her.

He dreamt about her often. She would always
be ahead of him, her back turned towards him
as she walked away, and no matter how hard he

tried he could never quite catch up. Sometimes he dreamt that his fingertips drifted over the fabric of her blouse, but it was never enough. She always slipped away.

And then he'd remember. What he'd said before he went down for surgery—his attempt to make her leave him. He'd been trying to save her. Save her from having to tell everyone the bad news. She'd had to do it for her parents and her husband already—did he really need to put her through that again?

But it had worked. The surgery had been a success. And when he'd woken from his anaesthetic and seen her standing there so stiffly, so far away both physically and emotionally, he'd been in shock. Unable to believe that he wasn't dreaming. That he wasn't in heaven and that the sight of her there wasn't just a cruel trick of his mind.

He'd had a death sentence. A one-way ticket to an early grave. And he'd accepted that future. For it now to be so radically different was confusing and scary, and lying in that hospital bed, staring at the almost too bright white walls, he'd wanted to reach out and hold her hand, tell her he was sorry. But he'd never got the chance.

He'd called her a few times from the hospital in the days that followed. She hadn't answered her mobile, and at the house Mhairi would answer and tell him that he couldn't speak to her. It was like trying to get past a guardian at a gate, or a bouncer at a nightclub—only in this case the bouncer was a little old lady in her seventies, armed with a surprising capacity for swear words.

His father had visited often and brought Rosie. He'd never been so happy to see his daughter. The last time he'd seen her had been at home, waving goodbye, believing that he'd said goodbye for ever, and yet here they were, reunited. And it hadn't mattered that she'd wanted to bounce around on his bed, or that she'd spoken really loudly and begged him to read her a story. It had been his pleasure, and he knew he would never take for granted a single second that he got to spend with her from now on.

No moving in with Grandpa Doug.

He had Keir to thank for that.

And Bethan.

He wanted to say thank you even if she wouldn't allow him anything else. He knew he'd probably broken her heart by saying what he had, but he hadn't meant it! She was angry with him. Hurt by him. But surely she would give him the chance to explain?

And he just might get that chance today. Bethan was scheduled to pay him a home visit in place of Dr McKellen, who was away. He needed his vitals checked. His wound checked and redressed. Though as far as he knew it was healing well.

He missed her. Dreadfully. Every time the hospital door had opened he'd hoped she'd walk through. Every time a nurse had said, 'I have a message for you,' he'd hoped it would be from her. Only it never was.

Perhaps it was time to accept that he'd ruined things? Irrevocably.

He'd wanted to live for a future with his daughter, but he'd also hoped for a future with *her*. There. He could admit it to himself. He wanted Bethan back. But had he hurt her so much she wouldn't be able to see past her anger and hurt?

He missed her smile. The way she determinedly bit her lip when she was thinking hard. The way her eyes twinkled when she found something amusing. Just the way she made him feel. There'd been no future for them before, but there was now, and surely she should give him the benefit of the doubt and allow him time to say he was sorry? To explain it all?

Cameron glanced at the clock. Eight forty-six a.m. She would be here soon. How could he look her in the eye? Would she even turn up?

Yes, of course she will.

Suddenly he felt afraid. Afraid that if he told her everything and she still walked away…

'I want to cancel Bethan,' he told his father in a panic.

'Don't be a dunderheid! You need your wound redressed.'

He'd not told his father the whole story. Why he'd gone into surgery alone.

'She didn't leave me, Dad.'

'Did she not?'

'It was me. I said something to her…'

'What kind of thing?'

'That bit's not important. She wanted to stay with me. She wanted to be with me to the end.'

His father frowned. 'So what happened, then?'

'I got scared. I couldn't bear the idea of her having to give the news of my death to everyone—she'd done that enough times with her own family—so I said something horrible to make her go. She didn't want to leave me, but I made her.'

He looked down at the bedspread, guilty. Ashamed.

He could feel the weight of his father's stare upon him. 'Are you telling me that she wanted to be with you but you got *rid* of her?'

Cam nodded.

'You great lump! You don't know how lucky you are sometimes.'

'*Lucky?* I had a death sentence hanging over me.'

'And yet you still managed to find a woman who wanted to be with you! Despite that, you great lummock! Och, I can't understand you young folk these days.'

'I'm sorry.'

His father looked out of the window at the sound of a car door being closed. 'Well, you need to tell *her* that.' He straightened his jumper and turned around. 'Because, she's here.'

Cam felt his heart begin to race in his chest. Bethan was here. He was going to see her again. Words couldn't express how he felt about that. It was so much more than nerves and anticipation and excitement and worry.

There were so many things he wanted to say to her, he wasn't sure what to say first. Start with an apology? Beg for forgiveness? What if she accepted his apology but still didn't want anything to do with him?

That would kill him. Her absence would be worse than any brain tumour.

He tried to sit up straight in his bed. He looked around the room, hoping it didn't look too much of a mess, but who was he fooling? Rosie had practically camped out in his bedroom since he got home, and the floor was covered in her books and toys and dolls.

It would have to do.

He would have to do.

His father was right. He had been a ridiculous fool.

CHAPTER TEN

SHE'D FELT SICK driving over. Her mind had kept coming up with all the different ways she could get out of this appointment—another patient emergency, perhaps, or a flat tyre. She had a migraine and couldn't drive… She had smallpox. Anything, no matter how ridiculous, just so she didn't have to face the man she knew she loved.

How stupid am I? Falling in love with a man who doesn't want me?

She'd spent the whole weekend telling herself how ridiculous it was. Falling for a man who was dying. *Dying!* Who would punish themselves in such a way? There had to be something wrong with her. She *liked* pain. She *liked* grief. Somehow she was attracted to it.

No wonder he'd got rid of her. He must have felt appalled. Thinking of her as some weird ghoul, entranced by sickness and death.

It didn't matter that she didn't really think it was true. The blind could not see.

Cam would hate seeing her today. He would be angry that Dr McKellen wasn't around to do this visit and that he would have to endure her.

Well, she wasn't looking forward to it either!

Now, Bethan glanced at his cottage, then away again. She felt sick. Shaky. Her legs were weak and wobbly. He would know that she was here. He would know that she was sitting in her car, not wanting to go in, and he would know that she was a coward.

It was enough to force her into movement.

Her mouth dry, she got out of the car and collected her bag from the boot. With dread in her heart she began the slow walk to the cottage's front door—a condemned woman going to the gallows.

Just do this quickly. In. Out. Then it'll all be over.

She hoped he would be congenial. Polite, if nothing else. But it would break her heart if he didn't look at her. Or say anything. This was going to be awkward for both of them.

Bethan knocked on the door, knowing that someone from his family would answer. Cam would be in bed, so who would it be? Rosie would be good. That sweet little girl whom she and Grace adored.

Instead Dougal Brodie opened it, and stood there looking at her.

Bethan looked down and away, before sucking in a breath and looking up again. 'I'm here on Dr McKellen's behalf,' she managed to mutter.

'Aye. Come in, lass.'

She frowned, a little put on the back foot, because this wasn't the greeting she'd expected from him. Hadn't she abandoned his son? Surely he'd be angry?

'He's upstairs. You know the way?'

She'd never been in his bedroom.

'I'll find it.'

She began to head up the stairs, feeling her heart begin to pound faster and faster at the idea of seeing Cam again. But before she got halfway up Dougal stopped her.

'He told me what happened. Between the two of you.'

Here it comes...

'I think he lost his mind for a moment there.' He shrugged. 'Fear will do strange things to a man...'

Bethan frowned, not sure what he was trying to say. When it became clear that Dougal wasn't going to say anything else, she continued to climb the stairs.

It felt like so long since she'd last seen Cam, but really it had only been a matter of a couple of weeks. She yearned for him still, no matter what he thought of her and that made her feel pathetic.

What kind of an idiot am I? An embarrassing sap.

On the landing at the top of the stairs she saw that only one door was open and sunlight streamed through from the windows inside. Tentatively she took a step forward and Cam, in his bed, moved into her view.

He looks amazing. Despite all that he's been through.

He looked healthy. Vital. Full colour in his cheeks despite the stark white dressing on the front of his head. He was looking at her with eyes filled with sorrow, which she guessed was better than anger, and so, with a slightly stronger resolve than she had felt since waking that morning, she stepped into his room.

'Hello, Cameron.'

'Bethan. You look well.'

'So do you.'

Look at how polite we're being with each other. Let's hope it stays that way and I survive this if I'm to walk away again.

'How have you been?' he asked.

Miserable without you. But how can I tell you that without you thinking I'm pathetic?

'Busy. You?'

Then she cringed, because of course he wouldn't have been busy. He'd been recuperating from the major brain surgery that had saved his life.

'I...er...need to check your dressing—is that all right?'

He nodded, never taking his eyes off her.

Why wouldn't he look away? Why was he watching her so intently? It was unnerving, and she could see that her hands were trembling as she opened up her bag and got out fresh dressings and her BP cuff and all the other paraphernalia she'd need.

'Is there a bathroom available? I need to wash my hands.'

What she actually needed was space to breathe. To gather herself. To get control of the shakes.

'The next room on your left.'

'Thank you.'

She practically raced from the room, shutting herself in the bathroom and leaning back against the door, fighting back the tears threatening to storm down her face—because she just couldn't bear this tense politeness they had going on between them.

It had used to be so *good*! They'd had such an easy manner between them. Had been able to talk about anything. Laugh about anything. And she missed that. Missed *him*. What she wanted more than anything else in the whole wide world right now was to sink into his arms, lay her head against his chest and have him hold her and stroke her hair, tell her everything would be all right between them.

She wiped her eyes and stared at herself in the mirror.

Get a grip!

Bethan washed her hands rigorously, dried them, and then checked her reflection one last time. Were her eyes still red? Or was it just the light in here? She took a deep breath and relaxed her shoulders, and then opened the door to head back to the bedroom.

Cam was still in bed. Waiting for her. Looking at her apprehensively. 'Are you okay?'

'Fine! Right—let's have a look at this wound, shall we?'

It was smaller than she'd imagined it would be. She'd half expected to see staples running in a half-moon over the front of his skull, but the incision was only about five centimetres in length and it was healing well. No redness, no signs of infection.

'These staples can come out now, I think.'

'That's great,' he answered.

She used a small tool that quickly and effectively removed the staples, dropping them into the small cardboard kidney dish she'd brought with her. Then she redressed the wound and removed the gloves she'd put on before beginning the procedure.

'Try and keep it dry for another few days, and then you should be able to wash your hair. Though do it carefully until you're fully healed.'

'Thanks. That'll feel good.'

'I'm sure it will. Do you mind if I do your blood pressure? Check your temperature?'

He nodded.

At least her hands weren't shaking any more. She was feeling emboldened by the fact that he hadn't attacked her verbally, or given her one of those looks, or treated her unkindly at all. And she could lose herself in the business of being a doctor. A place where she felt comfortable and in control.

'Bethan?'

She looked up and met his gaze. 'Yes?'

He looked apprehensive. Anxious. 'I...er... I need to say something.'

Oh. Here it comes.

Nausea hit her like a brick and she swallowed hard in a mouth that was as dry as dust. 'Right...'

His cheeks flushed with colour before he managed to make eye contact with her again. 'I…er… have to apologise. To you. Hugely apologise. If I gathered up every sorry in the world it wouldn't be enough to say just how sorry I am that I hurt you so badly. Appallingly, in fact.'

This was not what she'd been expecting and she stared at him in shock, her heart pounding.

'What I said to you in the hospital—I was scared. Scared not just for my life, and what was about to happen, but also scared for you.'

'Me?'

'Yes.' He let out a breath. 'You'd been through so much. What with your parents dying and then your husband. All I could see was you sitting beside me, knowing I might die, too, and I couldn't make you go through it again.'

His voice broke on the last word.

'It just felt so wrong, knowing that I was putting you through that, and I didn't want you to have to be the one to tell my daughter that I had died on the table. I felt that you would take the blame for putting me in contact with Keir and you would feel guilty for robbing me of my last few months with my daughter and...'

He looked up at her, a tear tumbling down his cheek. Met her gaze intently. 'I couldn't do that to you. I had to make you go. I tried to set you free.'

She stared back at him. Stunned.

'I tried to do it in the most awful way. By telling you I didn't love you. I lied, Bethan. I *lied*.'

Bethan stood up, unable to sit still a moment longer. 'You...' Her words choked in her throat. *He'd lied?*

He stared at her, hearing his bedside clock ticking away the seconds that passed in the silence.

'You lied?'

'Yes. I didn't mean it.'

She stared back. She was acutely aware that his father was downstairs, no doubt listening with one ear. Bethan looked away from him. Out of the window, across the lane and to the mountain that rose behind it in the distance. Mount Gillochrie, where they had first made love in the warmth of the early-morning sun.

He'd lied.

'Bethan? Would you look at me, please?'

She couldn't. Her mind was racing. Tumbling through all the confused thoughts she'd begun to have. If he'd lied to her then that meant that he *did* love her, and she loved him, and everything could be all right.

Couldn't it?

But she was scared. Trembling as she stood looking out of the window, her arms hugging her own body. The tears fell freely and silently. She didn't want him to see that she was crying.

She must have been in a world of her own. Because she didn't hear him get out of bed and pad across the floor to her in bare feet. The first she knew was his hot touch on her arm. She spun so fast, shocked that he'd crept up on her, that he had to grab her to steady her.

'I don't understand…'

'I was trying to protect you. From *me*. From the pain of my passing. That sounds incredibly arrogant, I know, but I thought if we argued, if you thought we weren't as close as we had been, then it would be easier for you, somehow.'

She needed some space to think. She couldn't

think clearly with him touching her. Not when she craved his touch.

'Easier?'

'I was trying to protect you, Bethan. Do you want to know why?'

'Because you pitied me?'

'Not pity, no. It was because I love you. And the only thing I could give you was my protection.'

Bethan stared. He loved her. Those were the words she'd dreamt of hearing. But now that he was saying them out loud, in real life, it was terrifying.

Was there the possibility of happiness after all?

'You love me? You're *in* love with me?'

He stared back at her, helpless and vulnerable to anything she might throw at him.

'Yes. I know I went about it the wrong way, but when you're faced with a death sentence and the depths of love at the same time, all you can do is try and protect those you love.'

She did know that. She *did*. 'You put me through hell, Cameron.'

'I know.'

'You hurt me.'

'I know. And I'll be sorry for that every day of my life. But let me make it up to you by being the best Cameron Brodie I can be in the life that you have given me. This gift that you have given me. You gave me everything back, Bethan. You fought for me, gave me life, and a future, and time with my daughter that I thought I would never get to enjoy.'

'Anyone would have done the same thing...'

'No, they wouldn't. You went the extra mile.'

'I *had* to.'

'Thank you.' He reached out and tentatively took her hands in his.

Bethan stared at him. He loved her. He was in love with her! Something she'd thought would never happen! And all that he had said had been a terrible lie. Could she forgive him for that? Could she forget it?

Time was a great healer. Wasn't that what everyone said? And his hands in hers felt amazing. She wanted more—to be back in his arms, where she felt she belonged. But she was afraid to tell him the truth. To tell him that she loved him, too.

'So what happens now?' she asked, looking

at him with tears in her eyes and running down her cheeks. She must look a sight, but she really didn't care at that moment.

'It's up to you. It's *all* up to you. I just had to be honest and tell you how I feel—even if you don't feel the same way as me. You deserve my honesty.'

'Right…' She nodded, feeling her heart racing in her chest like a racehorse thundering down the final straight. 'Only I do.'

He blinked and looked at her. 'What?'

'I do feel the same way.'

'As in…?'

She laughed. And hiccupped. 'As in I love you, too, you idiot! Why do you think I got so upset back then?'

He looked surprised, then a huge smile broke across his face and he pulled her towards him in a great big bear hug, squeezing her tight against his chest. She sank into it. Sank into the feel of him, the smell of him. The *wonder* of him.

She began to laugh, her smile broad against his tee shirt, as she hugged him back.

'Have we been *complete* fools?' she asked, closing her eyes in delight.

She had him back. He loved her and she loved him and they had a future. There was no tumour ready to strike him down in a few short months.

'We may just possibly have been the very worst of them,' Cameron agreed. 'We were scared fools. Terrified fools.'

She looked up at him. 'I don't ever want to be a fool again.'

'Nor me.'

He leaned in to kiss her. The warmth of his lips upon hers made her feel like sighing with contentment. Like purring with happiness. The cat that got the cream. Kissing him was everything she'd hoped it would be and more. She was home at last. And home was *everything*.

He squeezed her tight against him once more. 'I never dared to hope that you might feel the same.'

She laughed and held her finger up to his lips, silencing him. 'What matters is that there is a future for us. Together.'

'Definitely.' He kissed her again.

EPILOGUE

THE LITTLE CHURCH in Gilloch was filled to overflowing, with guests in their finest suits and dresses, hats and fascinators.

From outside, Bethan could hear them all chattering to one another as she organised her two flower girls, Grace and Rosie, into the correct position. Oh, and Hamish—Rosie's new Labrador puppy—who wore a bright red bow around his neck and seemed determined to remove it by prancing around and trying to eat it.

The girls smiled and giggled at his antics and she gave each of them a kiss on the cheek.

It had been a long six months, waiting for this day. But everyone was happy for them. Even old Angus Brodie, Cameron's grandfather, had come around.

Mhairi and Angus had got together at their engagement party and begun talking, putting the world to rights between them for the sake of their grandchildren.

It had taken Bethan some time to get used to the idea that she was going to get married again, but when Cameron had proposed halfway up Mount Gillochrie it had been a wonderful surprise! A memory she would cherish for ever.

Cameron had had a couple of check-ups with Keir and his scans were clear. There were no more cancer markers, so he was considered completely cured. He was just like any other man.

Except that he *wasn't* just any other man.

He was *her* man.

And she loved him more than she would have thought possible.

Bethan lowered her veil over her face and sucked in a deep breath. In a moment she would be Mrs Brodie. Dr Bethan Brodie. Working in the same GP practice as her husband and mother to two little girls.

Or maybe it would be *three*?

She had her suspicions. Something felt different, but it was still too soon to know.

Maybe she'd find out on their honeymoon?

They were going to go away to Italy. To a beautiful villa on Lake Como. The idea of telling Cameron she was carrying their child there lit her up inside so much she thought she would explode with light and joy. That so much life could come from so much darkness!

I'm ready.

She nodded to the usher and he opened the door. Inside she heard the music change to the traditional 'Wedding March'.

Grace, Rosie and Hamish stepped forward, perfectly in step, and the girls began to cast their rose petals.

And then Bethan stepped forward, too.

Into her happy and *long* future with the man she loved with all her heart.

* * * * *

LET'S TALK

For exclusive extracts, competitions
and special offers, find us online:

f facebook.com/millsandboon

📷 @millsandboonuk

🐦 @millsandboon

Or get in touch on 0844 844 1351*

For all the latest titles coming soon,
visit millsandboon.co.uk/nextmonth

*Calls cost 7p per minute plus your phone company's price per
minute access charge

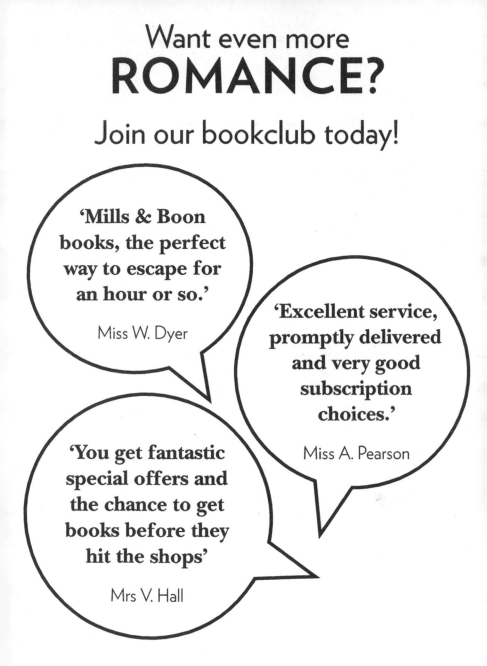